THE MONGREL

A St   nelle

of   s

b   ).

The Mongrel
A Story of Logan Fontenelle
of the Omaha Indians

Published by toExcel
an imprint of iUniverse.com, Inc.

For information address:
iUniverse.com, Inc.
620 North 48th Street
Suite 201
Lincoln, NE 68504-3467
www.iuniverse.com

Originally Published by South Platte Press

ISBN: 0-595-01087-3

This book is dedicated to the American Indian

Contents

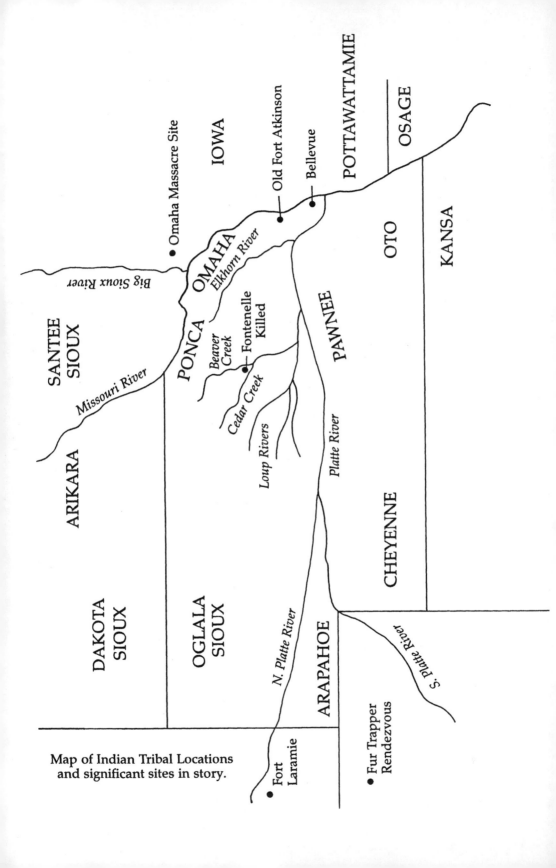

Map of Indian Tribal Locations and significant sites in story.

Preface

The desolate sandhills of the Nebraska prairie hold many tales of western history that never will be divulged. While living as a boy in Petersburg, one of the hamlets at the edge of this vast expanse of land, I spent long hours in an attempt to extract some of this history by making almost daily probes every summer into nearby hills seeking bones, pottery, and arrow points. These artifacts of a time long past, unrecorded, were intriguing enough to stimulate to the fullest the imagination of my youth. Each time I struck fortune in my hunts, the thunder of distant drums, the yelp of painted warriors, and the clank of war axes became as real to me as they were at the time they did indeed occur.

On one of these exciting adventures into the past, I happened upon a marker which read: "Fontenelle killed, 1855." This find was the impetus starting me on another long quest to identify the man called "Fontenelle," and learn why he had died on this remote plain.

The whole history of man's existence appears to be one of struggle, particularly against his own kind, and the experience of the Omaha Indian tribe in Nebraska is no exception. It is true that the large Sioux Nation suffered greatly in the wake of expansion of the white man's culture. But, as difficult as it is to believe, the Sioux were no more considerate of their red brothers (the Pawnee, Osage, Ponca, Arikara, Mandan, and in particular, the Omaha) than were the white prospectors of the rights of the Sioux in the gold fields of the Black Hills.

All of the early spoken and written history of the Omaha is honeycombed with accounts of unprovoked attacks by the Sioux. Most tribes of the West considered the mighty Sioux the "Zulus of the Western Plains," and none of them regretted the eventual demise of this great Indian nation. On the other hand, the continuous harassment conducted by the Sioux against the Omaha between the turn of the nineteenth century and the Civil War would lead any analyst to conclude that in some way the great Sioux leaders feared the tough knot of people who constituted the Omaha tribe. It was almost as if they felt that some day from the nucleus of this small group would spring a leader and a force to contest their supremacy in the territories between the Missouri River and the Rocky Mountains.

Even though actual accounts of his experiences are limited and unclear, leaving many gaps in the span of his life, the story of the bold, distinctive, and brilliant half-breed chief of the Omaha, Logan Fontenelle, the grandson of Big Elk, is the basis for this writing. The narrative, a historical novel, is a combination of fact and fiction and is an attempt to portray the incredible life and adventures of this outstanding personality-- who at times could be found in the dress of gentlemen negotiating treaties or the sale of tribal lands, and, who at other times, could be found bare-skinned roaming the remote Nebraska prairie challenging the dreaded Sioux. This work is also an effort to display the thoughts, feelings, and reactions of a young man who guided his people through extremely trying times brought on by encroachment of the white man on one side and by brutal pressure from superior forces of marauding Sioux on the other.

CHAPTER ONE

Source of Greatness

The Omaha Indian tribe of Nebraska belongs to the rather large Siouan linguistic stock. The original habitat of this stock remains hidden in the secret that surrounds the ancestry of the American Indian, however, it seems to have been located in the area of the Appalachian Mountains. Tradition states that in the early western migration of these people, they reached the country of the Great Lakes. One group of this original stock that kept together during this travel seems to have been composed of closely related people now known as the Omaha, Ponca, Osage, Kansa, Iowa, and Quapaw tribes.

Some time before 1541, it appears the people moved down the Ohio River finally reaching the Mississippi. At this point, the group separated, with one party moving downstream and the other upstream. This incident led to the names Omaha ("against the stream") and Quapaw ("with the current") by which these people are known to this day. The people who moved upstream eventually reached the Des Moines River and they followed it to its headwaters. The tribe in its wanderings seems to have lingered for periods of time in Iowa, North Dakota, South Dakota, and the upper Mississippi region of Minnesota. It was while in this latter region that the Omaha contacted the Cheyenne and made peace with them. The Dakota Sioux also made contact with the Cheyenne in their migration through Minnesota, but it is not clear if the Dakota had contact with the Omaha at that time.

About the year 1700, the Omaha occupied a large village at the juncture of the Big Sioux and the Missouri Rivers near the present day Nebraska-South Dakota border. It was from this point that the Ponca, Osage, Kansa, and Iowa broke off from the parent Omaha group for various reasons through the years, settling on lands up and down the Missouri River.

Photo of Logan Fontenelle taken about
1855--Published with permission of the
Douglas County Historical Society, Omaha,
Nebraska

While living in this village on the Big Sioux, the Omaha made contact with the Arikara who were living in earth lodges on the west side of the Missouri. Eventually Omaha war parties waged war on the Arikara and drove them northward along the river. The Omaha then laid claim to this land and it is this area that is partially occupied by the Omaha tribe today.

The Omaha first made contact with white men in the early 1700's. Tradition states that the major number of these men were French traders who built log structures and bartered with the people. Relations with these traders had an unsettling effect on the affairs of the tribe. The traders would give aid and favors to certain chiefs and leading men of the tribe and these Omaha would use the benefits to elevate their tribal standing. One of these men was the tall, handsome, ruthless Chief Blackbird, who loved the position of power and was very unscrupulous in how he obtained it.

The traders found out early that Blackbird could be easily manipulated to their advantage. They helped to promote his ambitions, supplied him with goods and taught him the use of arsenic as a poison. In turn, Blackbird allowed the Omaha to purchase the trader's wares at highly elevated prices. The Omaha did not complain and the traders became wealthy.

Blackbird convinced his people that the white men had made him a great chief with exceptional powers and he demonstrated these powers by eliminating his political enemies with the arsenic. Thus Blackbird became a highly feared, absolute ruler amongst his people.

Aside from being a despot, Blackbird was also a cruel warrior. Allied militarily with the Skidi Pawnee, Blackbird's warriors became a highly respected, formidable striking force. On one occasion, after the Ponca had stolen some Omaha horses, Blackbird pursued the culprits with a large warrior group to the main Ponca village. Twice the Ponca chief sent out braves carrying peace pipes, but Blackbird killed the emissaries on both occasions. Finally, the Ponca chief sent his young daughter carrying a peace pipe and only then did Blackbird take measures to make peace. In keeping with his reputed vile character, Blackbird kept the girl and married her. It has been said that she was his favorite wife.

Eventually, even Blackbird fell victim to the evil influence of the white traders. One day while consuming the white man's whiskey, he fell into a drunken rage and stabbed and killed the Ponca girl. One story states that in his grief, he covered himself with his buffalo robe and starved to death. To honor the chief, the Omaha buried Blackbird, sitting upon a horse, atop a commanding hill overlooking the Missouri. The hill came to be known as "Blackbird Hill" and served as a prominent landmark to explorers and travelers for many years to follow. The Omaha held the area as sacred and many important people of the tribe were buried in the vicinity.

Immediately following the Blackbird era, the size of the Omaha tribe became greatly reduced in size as a result of being ravaged by smallpox and continuing wars with the Sioux. When the people met with Lewis and Clark in 1805 while camped on Omaha Creek in northeast Nebraska, the tribe consisted of only one thousand men, women and children. The Omaha had reached the weakest point in their history; they were on the verge of extinction. They were in need of protection and they were in need of leadership, unlike that of Blackbird, that would provide the conditions of survival.

The period of time between the turn of the nineteenth century and the Civil War was a very critical time in the opening of the West. It was the heyday of the fur trader, of exploration of the Louisiana Purchase, of Indian feuds, and the exploitation of Indian lands. It was an unstable time, with the government struggling to secure its western holdings and with both settlers and Indians seeking security in a rugged land.

In 1819 Colonel Henry Atkinson headed an expedition up the Missouri consisting of 1100 men. It was the object of this party to establish a fort on the Yellowstone River in Montana in an attempt to neutralize the British influence in the area. At the time, Manuel Lisa operated a fur trading post some 20 miles north of present-day Omaha, Nebraska, on the site called "Council Bluffs" (not to be confused with present-day Council Bluffs, Iowa) where Lewis and Clark had sat in session with several tribes 15 years before.

When the Atkinson troops reached the Lisa trading post, they were beset with so many problems with their steamboats that Atkinson decided to build their fort at Council Bluffs. This fort was later named Fort Atkinson and it became the largest fort on the frontier. It is no wonder that during the brief life of this facility, the Omaha tribe took solace in its presence and camped nearby.

*   *   *   *   *

In the summer of 1833 Logan Fontenelle studied the wide sky and the horizons in all four directions from a high point on Blackbird Hill. As he scanned the distances, he concentrated deeply on the ways these various directions had figured in his existence and how, beyond a doubt, they would effect his future destiny. At age eight, Logan was well aware of his heritage. The son of an Omaha Indian maiden and a French fur trader, he knew he possessed unique characteristics, even though his mother had reared him only in the customs of the tribe.

Looking to the east, Logan tried to picture the huge lakes whence his mother's ancestors had migrated and the many hardships they had encountered in their trek to the west. Turning south, Logan recalled tales of how his father, Lucien, had left an aristocratic family in a large French city called New Orleans to seek his fortune in the unknown western wilderness. Up to this particular point, the young man's experience with the white man was all good. As he turned to the north, however, his thoughts were not as complimentary for his fellow redmen, the Sioux, whose attacks had produced great hardships for the Omaha tribe.

On a happier note, Logan turned to the west and smiled as he thought of the large buffalo herds grazing on the vast Nebraska grasslands in that direction. His nerves churned with excitement as he pictured the buffalo hunt which the tribe held once or twice a year to supplement its food supply. Ever since Logan was five years old, he had been promised by his mother that once he was mature enough, he could go on the hunt and possibly serve as a pony boy. Not only would the hunt be an exciting experience, but it was said that the trip acquainted young men with territories important in the future of the tribe and introduced them to friendly tribes as well as enemies.

Coming out of his meditation, Logan turned to Two Crows, a companion mounted bareback on a colorful pony nearby. "It's getting late and we should be getting home," said Logan as he climbed his mount and headed toward the place known as "Bellevue."

It was Bellevue along the Missouri River in eastern Nebraska territory that was the site of the tribe's last temporary encampment, the Indian Agency, and the trading post of the American Fur Company which was operated by Lucien Fontenelle. Also at Bellevue, Lucien had just finished building a comfortable log home for his family, and of this Logan was very proud.

The boys discussed the plight of the Omaha tribe as they rode. "You may not know it, Two Crows, but once our people were very powerful and our tipis and lodges stretched for many miles along this river valley," said Logan.

"If we were so powerful in the past, why does our tribe only have a thousand people at this time?" asked Two Crows.

"Our enemies, the Sioux, and the white man's diseases have carved the Omaha down to where we are today. I am scared when I see that we still face these problems. I don't know how much longer our people can survive them."

"We get along well with the Osage, the Oto, and others in the area, so why are we constantly at war with the Sioux?"

"Nobody seems to be able to answer that question," answered Logan. "The Sioux seem to have singled us out as their main target. Even our relatives, the Iowa, refuse to build their

villages next to us for fear of being destroyed by prowling
Sioux warriors."

It is historical fact that the Omaha tribe was not only
harassed by the Dakota and Oglala Sioux when hunting in areas
held to be communal by most tribes, but they were continually
subject to sneak raids as far east and south as Bellevue on the
Missouri. It was in this regard that Logan was proud of his
Omaha background. In particular, he esteemed his mother who
belonged to the Wehishte gens, a clan through whom the tribe
made known its displeasure over injuries from acts of other
tribes.

"Some times I believe that our people would have been wiped
out long ago if it wasn't for the spirit and guts of our
people," said Logan. "My mother is a good example. Once when I
was a baby, she discovered two Sioux braves in our lodge as they
were ready to put the knife to me in my crib. She grabbed a
hatchet and killed one of the braves and buried the ax in the
leg of the other as he fled out the window."

Continuing to the south, the boys soon neared what remained
of Fort Atkinson on the banks of the Missouri. It was here that
Logan was born and where his father made his home for the first
two years of Logan's life. When the fort was abandoned in 1827,
Lucien Fontenelle sought the protection of Bellevue as a place
to raise his family and conduct his business. Even though the
Omaha had some disdain for the white man, they felt relatively
secure in his presence. Hence a large contingent of Omaha built
a large village near Bellevue and the Indian Agency after 1827.

"Look at the size of this place! And it has just been left
to rot," said Two Crows in awe as the pair led their ponies
through the ruins of the former stockade.

"Life today sure would be much better for the Omaha if the
soldiers had stayed here," said Logan as he kicked in disgust at
a rusty, broken sabre in the dust. Remounting their ponies, the
pair moved homeward still deep in thought about the fort.

It was dark when the boys entered Bellevue, a boisterous community filled with trappers, explorers, pathfinders, and fur traders--all exemplifying the type of life prevailing to the north and west of this particular point. At his early age, Logan truly experienced life in the rough, continually exposed to all sorts of these rugged white adventurers who frequented the town. Generally a rowdy bunch, the frontiersmen often drank too much, fought among themselves, and on several occasions murdered each other.

Two Crows and Logan could hear the loud conversation in the drinking establishments as they rode their ponies down the rugged trail that passed for main street. "I think to avoid any trouble, we both should head for home," suggested Two Crows. "I'll see you in a few days." He then sped toward the Indian camp which consisted of several bark lodges, a few earth lodges, and many colorful tipis while Logan returned to the warm family home of his father.

In the house, Logan was greeted by his mother, three brothers, and a sister. Logan was never chastised by his mother for returning home late because she always encouraged the boys to imitate the Omaha braves and to learn to take care of themselves in the wild. Lucien, however, thought otherwise and sought to educate and train his children in the ways and finery of French culture. Even though Lucien felt this way about his children, he personally was far from being a refined gentleman, dressing in the costume of the frontier and often succumbing to the lure of alcohol like his fellow frontiersmen. Despite his gruff ways, Lucien was an intelligent, kind individual with great practical insight and a wealthy man because of his past daring exploits and business sense. Logan realized his father's good traits and he also recognized his own excellent lineage, putting much stock in the fact that his mother was the daughter of Big Elk, the Omaha chief who headed the Council of Seven Chiefs that directed the tribe.

Always eager to experience the thrills of life in his environment, Logan rose early the next morning and dressed to await his father's return from a venture down the Missouri.

"Good mornin' Logan," said Lucien as he hung his hat. "What brings you out of bed so early?"

"I want to talk to you about going along with the tribe on the buffalo hunt this fall," answered the boy.

As Logan spoke, Lucien shifted his eyes upward in obvious disapproval. Basically, he felt that Logan should be preparing himself for a future in the white man's world instead of occupying his thoughts and efforts with the problems and archaic ways of the Indian. Wisely, he sought to change the subject: "In a few days the new steamboat of the fur company will be landing here and it will be carrying a very famous painter, a George Catlin from Philadelphia. Why don't you go with me to greet him and ask him to stay here with us. If he accepts, it should be an exciting experience for the whole family." Immediately, the subject of the buffalo hunt was forgotten and the conversation led to discussion of how to entertain the great Catlin during his Bellevue stay.

The bank of the river resembled a carnival celebration as all the inhabitants of the area near Bellevue turned out to welcome the steamboat, Yellowstone, when it banked on a warm, beautiful summer day. Represented were the missionaries of several religions, Pottawattamie, Omaha, Oto, trappers, buffalo hunters, and several whites regarded as opportunists who might take up any profession in trade for whiskey, silver, or gold.

The drums of the Oto lent an air of celebration as the visitors came ashore and as the workmen began to unload supplies for the Indian Agency and the trading post.

Lucien stepped forward to welcome the captain of the Yellowstone who in turn introduced several government land appraisers, a Presbyterian clergyman, a whiskey drummer, and Catlin the painter.

Hurriedly, Lucien and Logan descended upon Catlin. "You are now on the frontier, Catlin," said Lucien. "The quarters here in Bellevue are not very good. If you are looking for a place to stay, your only choices will be a sod house, a bark lodge or a tipi. I have a very nice home for this outpost and you are welcome to stay with us for the length of your visit."

Catlin's face showed complete surprise and his mouth stood open momentarily. "Just think of it, a real bed to sleep in five hundred miles from Saint Louis!" roared Catlin as he willingly accepted.

Lucien pointed to Catlin's luggage. "Logan, strap those bags on the pack horse and let's take Mr. Catlin home."

Catlin's visit with the Fontenelle family was a delightful experience for all. The Fontenelles were both amused and awed by the talent of the man who sketched likenesses of the whole family and the beautiful setting overlooking the Missouri. "This setting is truly everything its name describes," stated Catlin on his first day in the field. "From a painter's standpoint it truly is la bella vue."

It is of interest to note here that not all visitors to Bellevue and the Indian Agency shared Catlin's views about the beauty of the place. For example, the nephew of Washington Irving, John Irving, Jr., who visited the agency in the 1830's, was anything but impressed with this outpost that was fast becoming the gateway to the West for the caravans of the fur trade and for the missionaries interested in converting the heathens to the north and west. In his displeasure with the Indian Agency and the trading post, Irving wrote: "It is made up of a half dozen rough structures inhabited by roughians who have full-blooded squaws for wives and a large number of mongrel children." Indeed, Logan and his brothers and sister were no doubt included in Irving's classification of Bellevue progeny.

In the days following Catlin's arrival, Logan and the other children recognized him as a true genius, yet they also were well aware of how naive he was of the rawboned nature of the West. They agreed among themselves that he needed a realistic indoctrination before they could let him venture further north where they knew conditions were strikingly more rugged and brutal than in Bellevue. They often speculated on how this slight figure of a man might fare in the camps of the Crow or Flatheads with only his pad and pencils and artistic nature to buy passage for his very life.

The highlight of the Catlin visit came on the day Logan and Albert led him to the Omaha camp. "I can't believe what I am seeing," said the painter. "The colors in those tipis are brighter than those in a professional painter's mix. And look, the women are doing all the work and the men are just standing around and talking!"

"Common labor is beneath the level of the braves," quipped Albert. "They spend their spare time with more important things than work, such as discussing defense of the tribe, war and hunting." On these words, Catlin shook his head in utter disbelief.

The party then sighted a married couple decorating the buffalo skins that eventually would compose the main cover for a tipi. Naturally this captivated Catlin's attention because both the man and woman seemed very skillful. The man outlined the design on the skin and the woman artfully filled in the colors with a bone marrow brush. The scenes depicted were taken from a vision which applied to the particular household or family. Catlin was so taken by this setting that he spent a good period of time putting the essentials of it on his sketch pad.

The party walked their horses up the main thoroughfare of the village, past the chief's pole and up to Big Elk's lodge. During this time, with glances left and right, Catlin gathered in a wealth of images and color quickly storing them for future use. Logan tied his horse to the lodge, paused at the doorway and then entered to summon his grandfather to meet his newly-found friend.

Big Elk stood at the door casting a very impressive figure with his great height, his dark, piercing eyes, short hair, long robe, and medals of authority. At his side hung a long knife, and a sharp tomahawk was positioned at an angle into his belt.

"Welcome to the village of the Omaha, Catlin," spoke Big Elk in perfect English. "Please come into my humble home and make yourself comfortable." The party filed inside the lodge and took seats on several large buffalo hides near a warm flickering fire where refreshments were plentiful.

The boys listened intently and in wonderment as Big Elk spoke to Catlin with in-depth knowledge of cities and leaders in the East. The chief was familiar with these people and places because of his visits to Washington where he had negotiated treaties between his tribe and the United States government. Highly elated and proud of their grandfather now that they were made aware of his experiences, the young pair's feelings turned to adoration as Big Elk spoke to Catlin of his high esteem for the Omaha people:

"Once the Omaha numbered into the thousands, occupying large areas of land to the north and east of this site. Disease and war, however, have carved us down to the one thousand that now occupy this encampment. We, the Omaha, have learned very harsh lessons from the past and what you see now are shrewd, keen and extremely brave people who are fighting for their very survival.

"The warriors of the Omaha are the best for this very reason. I would rather have these four or five hundred disciplined braves under my rule than the whole ragged Sioux Nation. Even as I am speaking to you now, my chiefs and braves are designing new methods of warfare. Although our people are few in number, I am having difficulty holding back the young men who are ready to spring forth to avenge the evils suffered by their fathers. Even though I have traveled far and have seen many things, I am still very proud to be the leader of these men.   I also am proud to say that in all the years that the Omaha have known the white man, not once has a member of this tribe raised a hand or weapon in anger to one of them, although many times it certainly would have been justified. This, I feel is a good record in view of the fact that most of the white men that we see are the worst in their society. Sincerely, Catlin, a white man of your stature is a real rarity and indeed a pleasure to meet. My people will be instructed that you have full freedom in the camp in order to pursue your distinguished work."

"You truly are one of the most influential and famous leaders on this vast frontier, Big Elk," Catlin said quietly.

"Would you do me the honor of sitting for me so that I can sketch you on my pad?" Agreeing, the veteran of numerous campaigns appeared quite natural as he adjusted his tomahawk and sat motionless for the painter.

Working feverishly, Catlin finished a good portrait of the chief in a short while. "One day this likeness will make you immortal, Big Elk, because I will hang it on display in the cities of the East to educate those people who do not know or understand the character of the people of the West," offered Catlin. Big Elk was delighted.

As the boys and Catlin left the lodge of Big Elk, Logan began to enumerate points of interest about the village and the various people within it. At a prominent place, as if to put them on display, the tribe had exhibited two large human skeletons side by side on a wooden slab. The skulls were alike, but of unusual shape possessing heavy brows, low frontal bones, and elongated occipitals. The total skeletons were over seven feet long showing extremely heavy arm and leg bones. Catlin was awed by this display. As he sketched the skeletons, he curiously inquired about their origin from the old men who passed by. The only answers he could obtain were those of pride, suggesting that the skeletons were ancestors of the Omaha attesting to the good stock from which the tribe was derived.

It was three weeks since George Catlin had arrived at the Bellevue landing and he was now eager to push inland for more adventure. Recognizing this fact, Bright Sun, Lucien, and all the children tried hard to convince Catlin that too many dangers lay to the north and west and if he ventured further his scalp was bound to wind up on the lodge pole of some Sioux, Blackfoot, or Crow brave. Catlin brushed off all of the persuasive talk of the Fontenelles and others in a final meeting where he gave his thoughts on the matter:

"Friends, before coming here my original plans were to travel through the most interesting parts of this country documenting what I see on my paper pads. I have not changed these plans. Even though I dread leaving you, I am sure that I will return and that will be another happy time. My plans from here are to travel to the lodges of the Mandan which lie along the Missouri to the north. Think of me as a messenger of peace as I go to paint and sketch and learn more about my Indian brothers."

No one could restrain Catlin any longer as he mounted a horse leading a pack horse which had been outfitted by Lucien. The sky was clear and the day exceptionally beautiful as Catlin waved to his friends from a distant hill. To the onlookers the excellent conditions seemed to serve as a good omen that the Catlin mission was destined to succeed and that he would return to Bellevue unharmed.

Life for Logan and his friends continued to be quite eventful as the warm days passed. More and more people were being brought into the area of Bellevue by the growing fleet of steamboats and keel boats the American Fur Company was using to expand its trade up the Missouri. Among the varied types of people traversing the area, the visit of the very dignified party led by Prince Alexander Maximilian of Prussia was indeed a highlight in Logan's life. The short, stocky Prince Max arrived at Bellevue with fifteen of his countrymen and two western scouts. The purpose of their visit was to catalog the flora and fauna of the area and also to hunt the famous American buffalo.

What a contrast these men were from their own hired guides and the other hunters, trappers, explorers, and traders who frequented the area. Logan and Iron Eye, his cousin who lived in nearby Bellevue, were drawn daily to the camp of the Prussians, attracted not only by their high shining boots, monocles, and powerful long rifles, but also by their swashbuckling mannerisms and guttural conversation. From some distance, the boys would stand wide-eyed and silent as they viewed this strange group maintain their gear, weapons, and animals for their exploit into the wilderness.

Each day they watched Maximilian writing and sketching pictures in his logbook and they could see another member of the group, a talented painter named Bodmer, making detailed paintings of the landscape.

One day, feeling motivated to learn more about these men and their mission, Logan approached Maximilian. "What are you gentlemen planning to hunt with those huge guns? My friend and I are good hunters; we would like to go along with you."

Prince Max stroked his mustache and roared with laughter at the impertinence of this lad who dressed like an Indian yet didn't completely look like an Indian. "What could you possibly hope to kill on a hunt with grown men?" he queried. "Perhaps you might snare a rabbit or two for some good hasenpfeffer, No?" Again the rugged Prussian roared with laughter.

"I am Logan Fontenelle and this is my cousin Iron Eye," said the young Omaha as he kept his composure. This completely astonished the prince. Who was this Indian with a French name that used the English language so fluently? So impressed was Max that he decided to show the pair around the camp and introduce them to his Prussian friends and guides. As the trio toured the camp, each member of the hunting party joined the group after being introduced, so that at the end of the tour the party consisted of most of the adventurers.

At this point, the jovial nature of the band allowed Logan a good opportunity for his next move. "I don't know if you realize it, prince, but your party is camped on my family's property. So, I am putting a fine on you for trespassing." On this, the area resounded with the heavy laughter of the adventurers. Everyone laughed except Max who for the first time in his life showed signs of embarrassment. Just who was this upstart of the frontier who was toying with his dignity?

"Your penalty will be that you honor my family with a visit to our home tomorrow evening," insisted Logan.

Relieved, yet somewhat bewildered by the whole incident, Max shook the hands of the boys and promised to call at the Fontenelle home as directed.

The occasion of the visit by Prince Maximilian was a real pleasure for the rugged but gracious Lucien. Bright Sun served

an excellent meal and the evening was spent with Lucien telling
tales of New Orleans and his numerous trips to the plains and
the Rocky Mountains where he traded for furs with white men and
Indians of all sorts.   Maximilian seemed more anxious to talk on
the subject of Indians and hunting than to spin tales of his
native land or his war experiences.

The prince left the Fontenelle home that evening a very
happy man.   He could not believe that such an unusual family
existed there in the wilderness and he was delighted at making
the acquaintance of Lucien.   Such a man would be invaluable in
briefing him on the supplies that the expedition would need and
the proper strategy to use in their exploration of the vast
wastelands to the north and west.   Another subject on which the
crafty prince knew he would need help was that of the safeguards
to take in order to survive on the sinister plains of the Dakota
and Montana territories.   Content for the time being, the
dignified Maximilian meandered slowly down the trail to his camp
fully absorbing the quiet of the spring night, the big sky, the
reflecting river far below, and the haunting beauty of the
forest around him.

As Maximilian approached the camp, he could sense that
something was wrong from the unusual activity for the late
hour.   Drawing closer, he could see that everyone was stirring
about and carrying weapons.   The medic of the group was
administering to a young, wounded Indian warrior and at the edge
of the clearing lay another brave about whom no one was
concerned.   He was dead with a hole from a long rifle clear
through his body.

"Two guards of the night watch caught these Indians stealing
horses and fired on them," explained one of the adventurers to
the stunned prince.   "Believe that one will live."

Moving to the wounded brave, Max observed the medic applying
the finish dressing to a wound on the thigh of the right leg
while the brave writhed in pain.

"It's only a flesh wound, but he will need several days of
rest before he can walk," noted the medic.   "With his fierce

attitude, however, he will have to be bound in order to mend properly."

"With that war paint on his face and that ax and knife in his belt, he's probably no friend. You'd better take his weapons and stake him to the ground," said Max.

As the medic carried out Max's orders and arranged a bed for his patient, the rest of the party gathered around discussing the incident and the identity of the two brazen redmen.

"I'm certain that they are not Omaha, but Lucien Fontenelle will give us a positive identification in the morning," stated Max. "Let's double the guard and get some sleep."

The next morning the adventurers found the captive sound asleep and apparently free of pain from the "universal anecdote" administered by the astute medic. Following breakfast, Max summoned Lucien to the camp and he arrived shortly thereafter. Lucien shook his head as he first viewed the dead brave. He then looked over the wounded warrior. As Lucien pondered, an expression of deep concern came over his face, which worried Maximilian.

"These are Oglala Sioux," said Lucien. "I don't like the situation this has created."

Lucien then spoke to the wounded brave with some fluency and the warrior answered him in apparent anger. The conversation raged for a time, with Lucien emerging with the same serious expression. He explained to the prince that the young man was "Sharp Horn," the nephew of Goes To War, a chief of the Oglala now camped some one hundred and fifty miles to the northwest.

"He is very angry that his friend was killed and that he is seriously wounded over two scrawny horses," Lucien reported. "He told me that he and his fellow brave had lost their horses while sleeping and they needed new ones to return to camp."

After serious contemplation, Lucien explained to Max that when the brave healed it would do no good to turn him over to the army at Camp Leavenworth because they would just free him. Even though Sharp Horn would soon carry the tale of the incident to the rest of the Sioux, and perhaps bring immediate or delayed retaliation, Lucien stated that the better alternative would be to free the warrior.

"If you can give him a horse," Lucien suggested, "and I explain to him that he is fortunate to be free and alive after stealing, maybe he will be less inclined to seek revenge."

Maximilian agreed and Lucien returned to explain the decision to the young but vengeful Sioux.

Max was very pleased on the day that he freed Sharp Horn and thankful that he had sought Lucien's counsel. He hoped that his own guides would be able to show the same wisdom once his party left on their big probe into hostile territory.

After the Sharp Horn incident, Max realized that it would delay his leaving by several weeks for he felt bound in conscience to stay and help defend the Fontenelle family and the Omaha camp should the Sioux attack to avenge the death of the young brave. He knew his war-experienced men and their fire power certainly would be a deciding factor should this happen.

The days following the release of Sharp Horn saw much defensive preparation carried out near the home of the Fontenelles and also in the camp of the Omaha. During this time, many of the young Omaha braves were able to practice some of their ideas of defensive warfare and some of them served as roving scouts to the west and north in order to give the people of the Bellevue community early warning in the event of the coming of the Sioux.

After several weeks, it became apparent that the Oglala chief, Goes To War, anticipated that preparations would be made for him and so he did not attack, possibly choosing to pick his own time and place for revenge. What had happened to the dead brave and Sharp Horn, however, should have served as an omen to Goes To War of what would befall the Sioux in their future dealings with the Omaha.

The preparations for war had been a maturing experience for many in the village of Bellevue. Logan and Iron Eye had learned one more lesson and the hunting party under Maximilian now felt it was better prepared to meet possible future dangers in this savage land.

Another maturing milestone was passed by Logan the day that Max and party embarked on the steamboat Yellowstone en route to their big adventure to the north.   It was like losing an older brother as Max waved aristocratically from the stern of the vessel.

"Come back to see me soon," shouted Logan, blinded by eyes full of tears.

"You soon will see too much of us," echoed the prince as the steamboat moved upstream.

Now more than ever, Logan dreamed of adventure and of joining the buffalo hunt in the late summer.   Each time the subject was brought up at home in the evening discussions, Bright Sun encouraged it, but Lucien always expressed his doubts and suggested that he seek advice from more experienced hunters such as Big Elk.

"I understand," the concerned father revealed, "that a very experienced frontiersman and hunter named Kit Carson has just moved into the Omaha camp from the land of the Iowa.   I suggest that you go consult with him about hunting buffalo and the dangers involved," offered Lucien.

Hearing this news, Logan was extremely elated and immediately began making plans to meet the white man with the great reputation.   All night Logan tossed in his sleep anticipating a glimpse of Carson and perhaps some conversation with him.

Logan rose early the next morning and without eating found his way to his cousin's home.   Soon he and Iron Eye were on the path to the Omaha village.   They passed the outer circle of lookouts and were waved on by this well-armed group of warriors.   Passing the inner circle of lookouts made up of young, eager braves, they were again permitted to proceed.   It was obvious from this showing of alertness that Big Elk was still anticipating a visit from the dreaded Sioux.   When the boys entered camp, there was little activity.   An American flag fluttered atop the chief's pole.   Sitting beneath the pole, a lone drummer beat out a peaceful rhythm--an outward sign that all was well within the camp.

Soon Logan and Iron Eye met Two Crows and immediately inquired into the whereabouts of Carson. "He is living in the lodge of his friend and fellow bachelor, Big Snake," said Two Crows. "It would not be good to disturb them at this hour because in celebration of their reunion they drank heavily and were boisterous well into the night. Neither will be in happy spirits this early in the morning."

Sitting near the lodge, the boys began a vigil hoping to get a glimpse of Big Snake and his famous guest.

The day was balmy and quiet and only a crow could be heard in the distance. Lacking sleep, both Logan and Iron Eye began to doze. Suddenly the skins covering the door opening of the lodge parted and out stepped the lean Kit Carson. His uncombed hair and three- or four-day growth of beard gave him a very wild, repulsive appearance that shocked even the sleepy eyes of Logan and Iron Eye.

Carson stumbled to a water pot near the lodge, removed the lid and plunged his whole head into the contents. He emerged after several moments, gargled and spit out a huge stream of water. With both hands on his head arranging his hair, he stumbled back into the lodge. From all appearances, Big Snake, an Indian who could not handle his spirits as well as Carson, was still asleep.

Soon Carson appeared again, this time wearing a large slouch hat and carrying a big knife in his hand. Moving to the water pot, he soaped his face for several minutes leaving the suds in place. Carson then sat on the ground and began hacking away at his beard with the knife.

Feeling that this was an opportune time to move in, the boys walked slowly toward the frontiersman. Before they could speak, Carson uttered: "This is one of the pleasures of life you damned Indians don't get to enjoy." Expecting no response, Carson almost opened his jugular as Iron Eye quipped: "The redman would rather remove hair from the top of the head than from the side of a rosy cheek." Carson roared with laughter until Big Snake groaned in his sleep.

"We'd better be quiet," said Carson.   "The Snake is drunk and may prove your point with that scalping knife of his." Suddenly, Big Snake stumbled from the lodge and followed Carson's steps to the water pot, also plunging his head into its depths.   After pulling out, Big Snake stood by the pot staring into space with his long, stringy, black hair dripping to the sand.

Carson studied the situation and then turned to the boys saying, "There's only one thing worse than a drunken woman and that's a drunken Indian.   They just plain lose their damn dignity."

CHAPTER TWO

A Taste of Seasoning

In the weeks and months that followed the meeting of the boys with Carson, the trio became very close through participation in games, conversation and short hunting trips into the nearby forest. Carson seemed like a big brother to the boys and he convinced them that to try to mature too soon could be disastrous and that they should enjoy the carefree life of youth as long as possible. "You'll be an adult with adult responsibilities soon enough so don't rush things," advised the plainsman who probably was forced to shift for himself too early in life.

One day in one of his meetings with Logan and Iron Eye, Carson caught the boys by complete surprise. "I'm soon to become a member of the family," he remarked. "Moneta and I plan to be married soon." The news placed the boys in total awe because they weren't even aware that Kit was seeing Moneta, the youngest and most beautiful daughter of Big Elk.

At the news of the engagement, the Omaha encampment became wild with excitement because it was well over a year since the last tribal party and the people were highly in need of a celebration to build spirit and morale.

On an overcast day in September, no one in the Omaha camp noticed how dreary it was because every one was making preparations for the marriage and the inevitable celebration that was to follow. The young braves began the day by arranging their costumes for the dance of the marriage feast. The older men were roasting various animals such as deer, swine, elk, and rabbit over open fires so that no one would lack food during the gala affair. The women kept busy preparing other foods and setting them out on tables and blankets so that these treats were readily available to all.

Carson and Big Snake arose early this morning to bathe and dress for the exciting and important event. Carson looked very handsome in a suit that had been set aside for important occasions and Big Snake made an impressive image in a beaded and highly decorated garb which also was reserved for occasions of this importance.

Moneta was beautiful in her rich white dress that was adorned exquisitely with beadwork and feathers by the women of the tribe. The bride's skin held no blemishes and her dark hair was gathered on each side in single ties hanging long and flowing. She was beyond a doubt the most beautiful woman in the entire area and a prize too good for most men in the territory.

The marriage ceremony was not conducted in the usual manner of the tribe because Carson's family was not represented. However, the rite was conducted in the lodge of Big Elk by the chief himself with the Council of Chiefs looking on as witnesses. The smoking of the Sacred Pipe by the groom, the bride's father, and the witnesses sealed the marriage in the eyes of Omaha law.

The hills around Bellevue had never before heard a celebration the likes of that which followed the marriage of Kit and Moneta. The Omaha drank and danced for two days. In Bellevue, it didn't take too much coaxing to stimulate a party mood among the trappers, loafers, hunters, and mountain men who composed the citizenry of the town. Also, the availability of bad whiskey ("rot gut") made the party a roaring success.

*   *   *   *   *

In the spring of 1837, it was decided that the tribe would be short on its summer meat supply. Consequently, plans were drawn up to divide the warrior force into two different hunting parties. One was to move west along the Platte River and set up camp some thirty miles from the Bellevue site. The other group was to extend itself up the Elkhorn valley to the north some distance from the junction of the Elkhorn and Platte Rivers. Each of the parties was to return home after three weeks in pursuit of elk, deer, and antelope. It was felt that a hunting trip of this size would fill the meat coffers of the tribe until the big buffalo hunt in the fall. Logan, Two Crow, and Iron

Eye, who were not of warrior class, were required to stay home because there was no need of pony boys on a deer and elk hunt.

Life in Bellevue and the camp was very dull for the trio in the absence of most of the young braves.

"It seems to me that little can be gained for us by watching the old ladies wash clothing and listening to the old men brag of past deeds," Iron Eye grumbled. "We should launch off on a hunt of our own."

"But we've been told to stay here and help protect the village," answered Logan.

Two Crows summed up the feelings of all three by saying: "It shouldn't hurt to hunt for a few days along the river to the north. We could show the tribe that we can bring home as much meat as any of the braves on the deer hunt."

It was a windy and cloudy day as the boys started up the Missouri with their well-exercised bows and arrows as weapons. The first day of hunting was not an eventful one and on the first night, some thirty miles from home, they had to call on supplies in their packs to sustain themselves. With the short supply of this type of food, the boys would be obliged to kill game the next day.

The second day, Logan woke before dawn and roused the others. The hunters positioned themselves on the ground of a wide-open grassy area and scanned the space between their position and the river. By sunrise no grazing animals had come into the range of their bows.

Two Crows broke the silence: "Looks like this is a lost cause. I think we should separate and take up positions in the trees and try to hit the deer taking cover for the day."

The hard scratchy seat in the limb of an ash tree was almost unbearable to Iron Eye keeping watch over a deer run just below his station. He lost all regard for his cramps and pain, though, as a large buck deer stepped into a nearby clearing. Nervously, Iron Eye fixed an arrow and took aim, but his arrow passed through the antler rack of the animal and in a flash the majestic beast was gone. The flow of terrible words that followed could be heard for a quarter of a mile away and it completely broke the setting, quickly bringing Logan and Two Crows to the tree.   The youths finally decided that it would be best to remain quiet the rest of the day and continue the hunt toward evening.

"We're not going to prove anything to the tribe about our hunting skills if we have another day like today," blurted Two Crows.   "I don't know about you but I am hungry and also kind of sleepy.   I think I'll just lie down on the cool bank of that creek over there and get some sleep."   The others followed suit with no coaxing.

After a couple hours of dozing, the trio was awakened by several fish jumping in the brook.   "Those are some good-sized fish!   Maybe we should try our luck at some fishing," exclaimed Two Crows, who was always prepared for the sport.   "I'll get the hooks and lines from my pony pack."

It wasn't long before the hooks were baited and in the creek.   Soon seven nice-sized catfish and carp lay on the bank. The three young men spent the rest of the afternoon building a fire, cooking fish, and feasting on their unexpected quarry.

"The shadows are already falling to the east," Logan remarked.   "I think we should move closer to the big river and set up our deer watch."   This time the boys remained together and anxiously took cover near an open grazing area.

Near sundown, as the young men remained quiet and motionless in their hiding place, the dead silence was broken by voices in the distance.   Filled with apprehension, the boys were petrified as they watched a large, heavily armed war party move into the grazing area and begin to set up camp.

"I believe these are Sioux, probably Oglala," whispered Iron Eye.

Fear suddenly struck the hearts of the young hunters as a Sioux brave rode his pony within a few yards of their hiding place.

"Why that's Sharp Horn riding the horse given to him by Prince Max to return to his people," whispered Logan angrily.

When Sharp Horn rode on and darkness set in, the boys returned to their camp where their ponies were tied.   Here they held a hurried meeting.

"This may be Goes To War's move on our village," explained Logan.   "Our people are in great trouble with all our braves on the hunting trip.   Two Crows, you ride to Bellevue to warn Big Elk and Iron Eye and I will try to find the warriors along the Platte and Elkhorn."

Packing hurriedly, the young Omaha rode hard in the direction of their respective destinations.   Uphill, downhill, through ravines and across plains, Logan and his cousin worked their horses.   With no concern for themselves or their animals, the young men had only one thought in mind--saving the people of the Bellevue community.

Our tribe is indeed very weak and it is demoralizing to have to run each time there is a threat from the Sioux.   Somehow, some way, the Sioux are going to have to learn to respect the Omaha and their lands, thought Logan.   The more Logan thought of the condition of the Omaha, the more he was spurred on in his ride to the Elkhorn.

The boys reached the bluffs overlooking the Elkhorn River just before sunrise.   "I don't see any camp fires, so the Omaha must not be here," said Iron Eye.

"I'll turn north along the river," said Logan to Iron Eye, "and you can go south to try to find the party hunting along the Platte."   Parting was a difficult experience for each, but both knew what they had to do.

Without rest for himself or his pony, Logan pushed up the river looking and searching.   By mid-day he paused to rest and give his pony a chance at the same.   Reluctantly, he fell into a deep sleep for several hours.

What a dangerous practice, falling asleep without concealing one's self, thought Logan as he woke.   I won't do that again.

It was now almost dark and Logan decided that this was a good time to continue because he could look for camp fires of the hunting party.   Moving up the river, the young Omaha came to a large creek that flowed into the river.   Knowing that the Omaha rarely camped on the banks of a large river, he decided to investigate a mile or so up the tributary.   He had traveled scarcely a mile when he sighted a fire with several figures moving about in the shadows.   Tying his horse, Logan crept closer to the fire to get a better look.   On first glance, he could see from the characteristic hats on some of the braves that these were Osage, relatives of the Omaha.   Immediately, Logan returned to his horse and rode slowly into the camp clearing.   With his right hand raised above his head, he shouted: "Osage brothers, I am White Horse, grandson of Big Elk.   May I enter your camp circle?"

"Come and rest and enjoy some of our meat," called Black Dog, the leader of the group.   Logan was hungry indeed, so he slid to the ground and moved toward the fire where the food was being prepared.   The grim-looking Osage warriors were very generous giving Logan large portions of deer and rabbit.

As Logan finished his meal, he was approached by the Osage leader.   "And what brings the grandson of the great Big Elk to this wild country?" queried Black Dog.

Logan was anxious to enlist the help of the Osage, so he briefly explained his presence in the area: "Late yesterday while hunting east of here, some friends and I discovered a large Oglala war party setting up camp along the Missouri.   With most of our braves on a hunting trip, I fear if they attack Bellevue all the whites and people in our camp will be wiped out."

"We've got to get word to the Omaha," cried Black Dog.   "We had a meeting with them two days ago and they are probably camped several miles north of here along the river.   The Osage will break camp now and we will escort you to your tribesmen."

Despite the dark, the Osage broke camp quickly and the party rode hastily to the north.   The older men stayed close to Logan to be sure that he wouldn't be lost during the rapid ride.   As the party moved along, Logan could tell that the Osage had no love for the Sioux and were sympathetic to the Omaha cause.   He also realized how simple it would be to recruit these excellent braves in a showdown with the Sioux, if and when the necessity presented itself.

An hour after sunrise, the Osage party and Logan rode into the Omaha hunting camp. They were greeted by Big Snake and Logan immediately explained his presence and that of the Osage. Hurriedly, Big Snake began the job of waking his warriors and getting them ready for a hurried trip home. Before leaving, he appointed six men to remain behind to pack and transport the meat from the hunt. The rest of the braves readied their weapons and began the move to Bellevue accompanied by the Osage. From Logan's description, Big Snake estimated that the Sioux war group probably was only two hundred strong, but he felt that a force such as that could overrun those in the town of Bellevue and the Omaha camp. The hunters knew that they would have to move quickly to save Bellevue from this horrible fate.

As the column of braves moved along, Logan knew that he could travel faster than the total party. Riding alongside Big Snake, Logan let him know what was on his mind: "I would like to strike out on my own. I know that I can reach Bellevue before the column and inform our people that help is on the way."

Big Snake nodded and Logan and his sturdy pony moved ahead of the long line of braves. Wildly, Logan rode across plain and valley, creek and wooded area, always moving in the direction of Bellevue and it wasn't long before he lost sight of the column of warriors.

Logan concentrated on how tired he was and how tired his pony must be, but on and on he pushed as the eager animal responded to his bidding, seeming to understand. Suddenly, before dark, the pony came up lame. Turning him loose, Logan continued on foot. It was a grueling experience as he ran and walked and ran again for many hours.

When the moon was high, White Horse reached a high point of ground. Here he sat down behind a clump of bushes, relaxed and fell asleep.

It was light as Logan awoke. Looking around he recognized a nearby creek as one which flowed toward the Platte River. Logan continued his pace along the creek's bank. After several hours, he reached a promontory from which he could see the Omaha village where everything appeared peaceful. Mustering every bit of energy in his body, Logan made a wild dash for the encampment. He dropped exhausted in front of the first lodge. As he fell many questions ran through his mind. Had Two Crows arrived home to warn the people? Where was Iron Eye? Had he found the other hunting party?

Two women soon found the collapsed herald, placed him on a bed in the lodge and summoned Big Elk. After a short sleep, Logan opened his eyes to face a smiling Two Crows and a sober-faced Big Elk. The worried look on Big Elk's face soon faded when he learned that Logan was fine and that the warriors would be arriving soon.

While Logan slept on, Iron Eye rode into camp with over a hundred braves from the second hunting party. In a short while Big Snake's band accompanied by the Osage entered the village.

Logan slept for almost a day and upon waking he could see the defensive preparations being made by the tribe. Viewing this, he decided to stay in the Omaha camp. He felt that his family was well protected in the Bellevue settlement and he also felt that his place was with the tribe, the real target of the Sioux.

*   *   *   *   *

It was a bright and warm day in the Oglala camp along the Missouri just eight miles from the town of Bellevue. This was to be the day of truth for the soldiers of the Sioux and particularly for Sharp Horn, who had an added cause.

Everyone in camp arose early, applied war paint, and rigged their steeds for battle. The war drum in the center of a large clearing began the rhythm for the Battle Dance. It was an emotional sight as the braves joined in the dance one at a time. A mere glimpse of this action would have struck terror in the timid hearts of many of the residents of Bellevue who were unaccustomed to the raw realities of the wilderness about them and who spent most of their time seeking the more pleasurable things in life, such as loafing and drinking.

In one hour the Sioux braves had worked themselves into a frenzy. They all appeared very stern and very intent on their mission. After a short while, the warriors mounted their steeds and in bristling fashion thundered out of camp behind their ruthless chief, Goes To War.

As the advancing Sioux battle force rode south at a high rate of speed, they suddenly were confronted by two figures that loomed in the path over which they were to proceed. One of these was a large man in clothes of the frontier with a long rifle across his arm. The other was a tall, thin man with flowing grey hair, heavy facial muscles, and tanned, leathery skin. He was dressed in a long black robe and was armed with only a large black cross. As the party approached, the pair stood firm raising their hands in peace. Goes To War rode forward to investigate, and as the column closed on the pair, he called his braves to a halt. Immediately, the chief recognized the duo and walked his horse slowly toward them.

"Why do you stand in my way, Blackrobe?" queried the chief. "Don't you realize that it would be easy for me to trample you into the sand?"

"Sioux braves do not attack men of God," said Pierre DeSmet, the Jesuit. Stunned by the nerve of the missionary, Goes To War had no immediate answer and merely stared into the distance.

The man in black continued his inquiry into the activity of the war party. "It appears from your haste and the direction in which you travel that you are moving on the Omaha!"

"You should be about your missionary duties and leave the mission of war to warriors," snorted the chief.

"What makes you think that Big Elk does not know of your presence?" asked the priest. "He may be waiting in ambush now to cut your relatively small force to pieces."

"Our scouts tell us that most of the Omaha braves are now hunting along the Elkhorn. Now is the time to strike and punish these scavengers who cavort with whites and threaten our lands. So stand to one side, Blackrobe, and let us be about our business."

DeSmet thought deeply. At all cost he must keep the Sioux away from the Omaha village. Quickly, he fired several rapid questions at the feared chief. "Are you telling me, Goes To War, that you are here to attack women, old men, and children who have been left behind in the Omaha camp?   Is this the heralded Goes To War, famous battle chief of the great Oglala? Has the reputed chief become so diminished that he now feeds on women and children?   Tell me, powerful one, how many scalps of old men will you hang on your belt today?"

Obviously embarrassed by these queries, the Sioux leader paused briefly, turned his mount around, and slowly rode to the north followed by his war party which included a very angry and frustrated nephew, Sharp Horn. Undoubtedly this was the first time in history that anyone had produced a Sioux retreat with a mere barrage of words.

*   *   *   *   *

After an alert vigil of almost two days, the braves of the Omaha were about ready to relax when they suddenly were alarmed by the sight of a tall, black, sinister-looking figure standing on a high point in the hills to the north of the village defenses.   Motionless, the figure appeared to analyze the unusual arrangement of the defenses below.   After several suspenseful minutes, the black figure was joined by a larger man dressed in skins and furs of the frontier. Following some conversation, the two men moved down the long slope and onto the flats toward the Omaha. Most of the Omaha felt that the appearance of the strangers could be a Sioux trick, so an air of uncertainty fell over the people in the defenses. They all realized that one volley from their guns could wipe the strangers out, but everyone remained very tight. No sign of peace was given by the oncomers and no one wanted to be the first to fire.

"It's DeSmet, the Blackrobe," bellowed Big Snake and the tension broke as several of the young men ran out to greet the

Jesuit. They ushered the missionary and his companion, a French mountain man named Louisiana into camp where DeSmet asked to see the chief, Big Elk. Logan and the rest of the young men followed closely observing every move of the great and famous Jesuit who had lived in the camps of every savage tribe to the west and north armed only with his cross and his holy face. When they reached Big Elk's lodge, the chief emerged and greeted the man in black with a friendly embrace. Even though DeSmet was also cordial, the grim look on his face was a concern to Big Elk as they entered the lodge. Once comfortable inside, Father DeSmet informed Big Elk of his contact with the Sioux and how he had convinced them to withdraw.

"It distresses me very much that my brothers, the Omaha and the Sioux, should be so hostile to each other when there is so much to share through cooperation," said DeSmet.

"We were well aware of the presence of the Oglala to our north," blurted Big Elk. "These invaders were here on a mission of vengeance, but we were ready for them. It is too bad that you have sent them away. They were small in number and if they had attacked, we would have cut them into buffalo jerk. It is time that we have taught these raiders a lesson. One of these days without the interference of Christians, as yourself, who feel that the Sioux are created in the image of goodness, we will send the Dakota and the Oglala back into their hills full of pain and mourning their dead. Father DeSmet, you are a holy man and you have spent many years among these people to the north, but you cannot condemn my people for defending themselves. Perhaps you can answer a question that has bothered me during my whole long life. Why have the Sioux committed so many offenses against my people? Why is it their vocation to attack and badger us?"

"The Omaha have been considered as intruders by the Sioux ever since they came to the Missouri to live many years ago," explained DeSmet. "The close relationship now between the white man and the Omaha has not helped to ease the situation. For scores of years the Sioux have lived with the philosophy that opposition is needed for tribal unity, hence to have an adversary is a way of life. Through the years, I have tried hard to instill principles of Christianity in the young people of the Sioux Nation. Until I can undo old customs, I am afraid that trouble will continue. The Sioux Nation is very large and unless Christians as myself become an influence in their activities, the wars are bound to go on."

To be polite, Big Elk nodded his head in apparent approval although he was not one to buy the Christian attitude toward tolerance. DeSmet issued his farewell to the chief and headed for the Bellevue settlement where he continued his business of hearing confessions, blessing marriages, and visiting friends.

The evening the Fontenelles entertained the Blackrobe was a very happy reunion. DeSmet had not visited in the Bellevue area since he had baptized the Fontenelle children and he marveled at how they had matured in his absence.

During the evening while seated in front of a comfortable fire, the family sat in amazement as DeSmet and Louisiana told stories of their most recent trek into the wilderness and their visits to the camps of the Mandan, Dakota, Oglala, Hunkpapa, Shoshoni, Crow, and Blackfeet. The priest told of the beautiful lands, of powerful warriors, of strange dances and customs among the people of these tribes.

Louisiana, who was gentle despite his huge size, frontier dress, and rugged mannerisms, captured Lucien's attention and interest.

"On many occasions, as we approached the camps of the hostiles, they would completely surround us, capture us, and then set us free to carry out our good work," said the big man. "Our reputation spread from tribe to tribe, even between people at war with one another. After a time, we were welcomed in strange camps with no introduction."

"Even though we encountered a diversity of religions, all the tribes seemed to understand our mission in that we were men of peace representing God. Toward the end of our series of visits most of the tribes offered protection to us as we moved through that vast territory. The trip was indeed a fabulous and unbelievable experience--far beyond the imagination of most white men."

The topic of conversation changed toward the end of the visit to the children and their educations. "I firmly believe that it is about time that Logan and Albert receive some formal schooling," spoke DeSmet.

"I feel that a knowledge of languages and mathematics is essential in the development of our young men and that would be important to the tribe as well," Bright Sun added. Lucien concurred.

"Well then, it is agreed that in my next visit here I will take the boys and enroll them in the Jesuit school at Florissant near Saint Louis," the Blackrobe concluded.

The outcome of the visit was much to the liking of Lucien who always had believed in a formal education for his children and was willing to pay for it.

CHAPTER THREE

A Dash of Bitters

With the spring hunt cut short, the people of the Omaha soon felt the need for meat again in the early days of summer. Once the maize and other crops were planted, the Omaha began hustling preparations for a summer buffalo hunt. For this particular excursion, the Council of Chiefs picked the director of the hunt, a young but capable warrior named Little Chief.

Almost every action of the Omaha had a religious connotation and the buffalo hunt was no exception. Probably more religious ceremony was attached to this than to any other activity. As a consequence, the man picked as the director would spend many hours preparing himself through prayers to Wakonda because the welfare of the tribe depended on the success of buffalo hunting. In the case of the Omaha, divine assistance was sought to ensure the safety of the hunters not only from the buffalo, but also from tribal enemies.

Logan and his cousin Iron Eye made plans to accompany the family of Two Crows on the hunt because their families were not to participate in the great quest. The three boys were extremely excited on the day of departure. They arose very early and had their ponies packed long before the adults were ready to move. It was the plan of the hunt to move west along the Platte River and then to seek buffalo in the area one hundred fifty miles to the northwest. Individual groups moved out heading for the site where the first night would be spent. When the last family had pulled out of camp, Little Chief followed the long column on foot as part of the religious ritual. It was his duty as hunt director to lag behind the tribe praying for the success of the venture. He wasn't expected to catch up with the tribe until late the first night after the camp had been set up and dinner prepared.

On the hunt, the tribe lived in brightly-colored tipis. The tipi covers and poles were used to construct travois which, when pulled by horses, represented the main mode of transportation in the cavalcade as it moved along the river. The men and women either walked or rode depending on each family's supply of horses while the children rode either on the travois or on pack horses with the household supplies.

The thrill ran high among the boys as they rode with the hunters and "soldiers" who kept law and order during the trek. The older braves broke the boredom of the long slow ride by jeering at the trio who were attempting to appear as hardened veterans of the trail.   The braves spared no punches in intimidating the boys.   Hard Hand, who was the most vocal amongst the soldiers, was particularly caustic: "Look who we are riding with, 'the official rabbit hunters' of the tribe, who almost starved to death on their last hunt."

Hearing enough, the boys soon fell behind to ride with another group that was their own age and that was more receptive to tales about their last adventure into the wilderness.

Camp was set up the first night along the wide and shallow Platte.   The occasion was one to remember with the flickering camp fires reflecting in the moonlit river and the long rows of tipis silhouetted against the broad star-studded sky.   Life at this point was a mysterious adventure that in the minds of the boys never would end.   Resting on their blankets, they remained awake until Little Chief arrived in camp, finally falling asleep along the splashing river as they talked of the adventures tomorrow would hold.

The tribe crossed the wide Platte the next day and continued their march west.   While camped in the evenings, the women would gather wild turnips that were peeled, sliced, dried, and sewn into bags of skin to be taken home for winter needs.

After a few days, the tribe crossed the Platte again and eventually reached the valley of the Loup River.   In order to avoid contact with the Pawnee, the Omaha then moved north into the hills of sand, the home of the buffalo. Precautionary measures were taken to hold down disturbances on the first stop in the sandhills. The women erected their tipis in a tribal circle and the tents housing the Sacred Pole and the White Buffalo hide (the symbol of successful buffalo hunts) were set up in their proper places. The soldiers were called by the hunt director to the tent of the White Buffalo where they were reminded of their duties. They were to prevent noises such as barking dogs or loud calls and they made arrangements to see that no one left camp on his own to hunt buffalo, for which the penalty was death.

The camp appeared very unusual the first night in the sandhills because for the first time on the trip it was not nestled in trees. Instead, it graced the rolling, grassy prairie that was pocked here and there with small erosions called "blow-outs." Sentinels were placed around the camp at some distances and camp fires were almost nonexistent because of the lack of wood.

Early in the morning, some twenty runners gathered at the tent of Little Chief to obtain their orders in the search for bison. These runners were not braves or even hunters, but young men ranging from sixteen to eighteen years of age.

"It will be your job to fan out in all directions and search for a herd that will furnish the tribe with a good supply of meat," spoke the hunt director. "I don't want any of you out there during the extreme heat of the day, so be back here by mid-afternoon. May Wakonda move with you in your important task."

The camp settled down awaiting the word on the bison once the runners had deployed.

It became very warm as the day wore on and it was difficult for most of the Omaha who were not used to life on this torrid plain. Many hours passed and by mid-afternoon the runners returned with stories of the lack of buffalo in the area. With these reports, the director ordered the tribe to make plans to move early the next day. Little Chief felt a bit apprehensive

over this new move because it would take the tribe closer to the
hunting lands claimed by the Sioux, even though they were held
as communal by all other tribes of the area.

The next morning the cavalcade pushed in a northwesterly
direction and the day wore on very hot.   Finally, at
mid-afternoon, the tribe reached a small stream meandering
through the sandhills.   Little Chief decided at this point to
make camp where there was some wood and plenty of fresh cool
water.   About three hours before sunset, Little Chief called for
a group of runners to range out only a few miles seeking
buffalo.   Some of the runners were back in camp before an hour
had passed telling of a large herd of bison grazing in the
direction of the setting sun.   Runners who had ranged to the
north had not seen buffalo, but reported seeing two riders
moving to the east.

Extra precautions were taken that night to hold down noises
and light in order to avoid frightening the buffalo and to
remain inconspicuous to the Sioux.   No fires were lit for the
preparation of food and the marshals were ordered to shoot any
barking dogs.

Everyone was restless through the early morning hours
anticipating the excitement of the impending hunt.   It was
certain that there would be buffalo because of the luck of the
runners in spotting the herd.   This fact added to the
stimulation of the youngest hunters who would participate in the
"surround and kill" for the first time in their lives.

The hunters were all prepared a short time after sunrise and
Little Chief awaited them at the tent of the White Buffalo.
There they received final instructions from the youthful
director and moved out following the two runners who had
discovered the herd.   The runners carried the Sacred Pipe,
another religious symbol of a successful hunt.   When the herd
was visible, the runners went to opposite sides of the grazing
animals meeting at a point on their far side.   The braves began
the surround on a signal from the hunt director slowly walking
their ponies into good positions to begin the chase and kill.

As the hunters moved into position, the women and boys came up to prepare to butcher the animals that would fall.

Little Chief gave the signal to attack with a wild yelp. From behind each dune of sand, the hunters poured into the dale where the animals were grazing. Riding bareback, they pushed their ponies at full speed toward the feeding beasts. At the first sight of the hunters, each animal suddenly became a horrendous momentum of hoof, hide, horn and hair. Many young hunters paused too long and missed their chances as the herd burst with awesome mass and speed. The more skillful men moved in close astride their fleet-footed steeds and with rifles cracking and arrows hissing they brought many of the bulls crashing down on the grassy sand. In a matter of a few seconds it was all over. As the dust settled on the long blades of grass, carcasses of brown dotted the plain, some still kicking in the last throes of life.

Appointed pony boys moved from bull to bull shortly after the kill, cutting out tongues and hearts--food for the sacred feast that would follow. The successful hunters celebrated by slapping at each other and swapping stories of their individual kills. Such was the privilege of the hunters and warriors, but the rest of the tribe had to work feverishly to dissect the dead animals and carry the meat and hides to camp for further processing.

Although the meat secured was not enough to call an end to the hunt, that evening there was great rejoicing and the tribe celebrated the sacred feast of the buffalo kill. In their elation the Omaha lit fires and the usual security procedures were abandoned. Everyone danced and ate late and as morning dawned, many slept where they had fallen from exhaustion. Luckily for the people, no prowling enemy had passed through the vicinity that night.

Upon rising, the tribe rested and passed a quiet day scraping hides and salting and drying meat. The young boys of the tribe took full advantage of the time off and spent the day swimming in the clear, cool creek. The heat of the sun, the

clean sand, and the fresh water were real delights to suit the
fancy of any lad the age of Logan, Iron Eye, and Two Crows.

The next day, the hunt director dispatched runners again in
all directions to find more buffalo. They returned near noon,
but none had sighted bison--not even survivors of the last
herd. With this news the tribe made plans to move and continue
their march into buffalo country.

Late in the morning of the second day on the move, the
forward scouts returned to the main body of the tribe at top
speed. They reported that they had made contact with scouts of
another tribe, non-Siouan, and that one of the leaders in that
scouting party had suggested a conference with the Omaha.

Immediately, Little Chief met with some of the elders and it
was voted to hold session with the other tribe.

The Omaha continued to move on with the warriors riding
abreast of each other forming a protective line in front of the
rest. The elders and the hunt director formed a group in the
middle of the front line. There they decided that Great Eagle,
a sub-chief, would speak for the people.

The day was humid and hot and the sky clear. The
anticipation of the forthcoming meeting seemed to make things
even warmer. After some three miles of travel, the monotony of
the hills suddenly was broken when about two hundred warriors
appeared on a long ridge in front of the hunting cavalcade.

Great Eagle recognized them immediately. "These men are
Comanche, a people we have had contact with before, but never in
war. It has been said that the first time the Omaha had seen a
horse in earlier times, it was ridden by a Comanche."

Great Eagle, an intent-looking man, rode toward the chief of
the Comanche accompanied by two elders. On halting, he drove
his lance into the ground as a sign of peace. On this sign, the
youthful Comanche chief dismounted.

"Hand me the Scared Pipe," said Great Eagle to one of the
elders. Receiving it, the chief slid off his horse, sat in the
grass, and began the process of filling and lighting the pipe.
Impressed by the moves of the older leader, the young Comanche

chief, Light Horse, followed suit and sat facing Great Eagle. The two leaders passed the pipe back and forth for some time before any words were exchanged. The Omaha chief broke the silence: "You have requested a meeting with us and we come with our weapons lowered because we recognize you as Comanche, a people who have never preyed on the Omaha."

"We Comanche have no quarrel with the Omaha and we seek your help and friendship," said the war painted chief. "I have led these braves here in search of five Comanche children stolen by renegades who fled into these hills. Not only have we been unable to find the children and their abductors, but we are out of food and my braves are hungry. I am here to help you in hunting the buffalo in exchange for enough meat to see us back to our people camping south and west of here."

Great Eagle stood and offered his hand to the Comanche who also jumped to a standing position. "The people of the Omaha are happy and flattered to accept your offer of help. Wakonda has been good to us and we have plenty of food to which you are welcome. We will worry about hunting later. Right now you are hungry and you need your strength." The Omaha sub-chief ordered his people to make camp and to break out some food supplies for the rugged riders from the southwest.

Great Eagle's decision was an expensive one, but he looked at it as a good investment. This move not only offered a chance to gain the friendship of the Comanche, but it would also help to deter any Sioux battle force that might be in the area, thought Great Eagle. Certainly the Sioux would not be foolish enough to attack the full force of the Omaha supported by two hundred Comanche.

Some of the Omaha did not feel the same way as the chief and they were heard to grumble. The young Comanche, however, were found to be very humble and polite and made many friends among the tribe. They accepted their food gratefully and set up their camp a short distance from the Omaha. That night the people slept with a feeling of greater security because of their new-found ally.

The combination of the Omaha and the Comanche was very successful in the days that followed in acquiring buffalo meat and the Omaha learned many things about horsemanship and riding from their friends.

The day the Comanche decided to return to their people was a sad one indeed for many of the Omaha because good friends had been made among the strong and eager young band. The Comanche mounted their horses and in a salute to the Omaha, circled the camp three times riding at top speed and in reckless abandon. What a thrill it was for the young Omaha boys as they saw the riders leave in true Comanche style. With true envy they watched until the last of the swift band disappeared over a distant sandhill and even until the last of the dust of their path settled to the ground. Oh, how Logan, Two Crows, and Iron Eye wished that they too could be off to high adventure with the independence of this nomadic pride of the southwestern plain.

Facing now the more mundane tasks of life, the Omaha packed for the long trek back to Bellevue. With the meat either dried or salted, the heavily-laden column moved southeasterly toward the Platte Valley. Little Chief allowed his people to rest in the middle of the day, traveling only in the mornings and evenings to avoid the heat of the summer days. When the column advanced, scouts were placed out at some distance from the tribe to warn against any impending danger. Fires were kept at a minimum at night, but no matter how inconspicuous the cavalcade tried to remain, the serenade of roving packs of coyotes or inspection from an occasional wolf seemed to indicate that the presence of the Omaha and their cargo was no secret. On the fourth morning of the homeward journey, the tribe meandered toward a row of bluffs indicative of the fact that they were nearing the Platte valley. The lethargic column was suddenly startled by several of their scouts moving in from the left side and waving crazily as they rode.

"Move the people into a defensive circle," ordered Great Eagle. This placed the women and children and pack horses on the inside and the mounted braves in a protective ring around them.

"A large Sioux war party is approaching from the direction of the bluffs!" shouted one of the scouts to Great Eagle as his party reached the defensive perimeter.

"Rig yourselves for battle!" Great Eagle ordered his lieutenants who were nervously standing by.

The element of surprise gone, the raiding Sioux drew up on a sandy hill above the Omaha. A siege at this point would be out of the question because the Omaha could outlast us with their supply of meat and water, thought the Sioux war chief as he analyzed the tough and tight defense below. Even though they are well fed and outnumber us, I wonder how willing they are to fight.

With one forward motion of his muscular arm, one hundred Sioux braves swept down the slope screaming their distaste for the defenders below. The war whoops and yells struck terror in the hearts of the women and children in the circle who cried in near panic, but the mounted Omaha braves held their ground. As the wave of Sioux skirted the circle, the bowmen of the Omaha sent arrows into the chests of two attackers and killed the horses of three others who went scurrying back to their friends at the top of the ridge. Logan and his friends watched wide-eyed from the under side of a travois as the Sioux turned, regrouped, and rode past the defense circle a second time, showering it with arrows and lances. This action brought flesh wounds to several of the Omaha braves and to some of the women, bringing even more fear to the people within the defenses.

Great Eagle decided to display some prowess of his own to instill more confidence in his warriors. While the fast-striking contingent of Sioux returned to the high ground, about fifty Omaha braves moved out and away from the circle and with war clubs and lances raised high, the band shouted insults and challenges to the Sioux perched on the elevation. Adding even more insult to the demonstration, the Omaha scalped the dead Sioux who were lying face down in the sand and waved the bloody hair locks at the onlooking marauders. The Sioux chief realized from this stroke of boldness that in spite of his mobile advantage, the defenders intended to fight.

Provoked by the gall of Great Eagle, the Sioux war chief threw his full force against the Omaha. The nomads careened at full speed down the slope into the bristling defense. One of the Omaha felled the leading brave with a long rifle and suddenly a tremendous roar arose as the cavalry forces met head on. Screams, cries, and war yells filled the valley as arrows, lances, axes, and war clubs found their marks. A horrifying sight resulted as human and horse flesh were thrown against each other and as the sand turned brown and red from bodies and blood.

The strength and brotherhood of the Omaha began to show shortly after the fight began. The Omaha never gave up. If they were knocked from their horses, they worked together to drag down enemy riders and kill them on the ground. The skill of the Omaha bowmen was superior to that of the dauntless Sioux and the ability of the Omaha braves with the war clubs soon proved that practice, not reputation, won the duels. The Sioux finally realized that they were not only facing the Omaha, but fighting an enemy that was sliding laterally and attacking from the rear. Seeing what was happening to his forces, the Sioux chief gave the signal to withdraw to the hill. As the Sioux soothed their wounds at their original point of attack, the Omaha hurried to regroup by carrying their wounded into the defensive circle, gathering fallen weapons, and rounding up loose horses.

Feelings were mixed among the people. The women and children in the circle grieved for their dead while an elated elder slapped Great Eagle on the back shouting: "That was great work. There must be twenty Sioux lying there in the grass!"

Once in formation again, the embattled Omaha braves shouted challenges enmasse to the quiet, trimmed down body of Sioux, waving their bloodied war clubs in added defiance. "Taste the bad medicine, you sons of vultures," bellowed Red Dog, the warrior, as he swung his tomahawk above his head.

The Omaha braves braced themselves again as they saw the long string of Sioux begin to stir. Much to their surprise, however, the movement was not another attack, but a withdrawal to the northeast. This puzzled Great Eagle. Surely the Omaha defense, although very good, was not enough to discourage the fearless Sioux, thought the chief.

The entire Omaha tribe stood in awe as the Sioux column veered away. In a few minutes it was obvious to everyone why the Sioux had withdrawn. Two hundred Comanche crowded the hill to the south where the Sioux had stood just minutes before. A tremendous cheer arose among the Omaha as the Comanche riders sped down the slope and encircled the Omaha who were still stunned by the sudden change of events. Women, children, and warriors broke from the circle and hugged their more than welcome friends. Great Eagle smiled as he greeted the young Comanche leader. The kindness and generosity of the Omaha sub-chief had just paid great dividends, making him feel very good inside and silencing his grumbling opposition for all time.

"After leaving your company, we decided to continue our search for the missing children for a short while," explained the Comanche to Great Eagle. "With our scouts fanning out in all directions, we soon found that you were under attack," said the young chief. "We came as quickly as we could to help our Omaha friends." These words put a warm feeling in Great Eagle's great fighting heart.

The rest of the day was spent in prayer for the nine Omaha braves who were killed in the fighting. Special attention was given to each one as they were laid out side by side in the grass and cactus. As he viewed the dead, Logan spoke their names silently. Hard Hand, Little Hawk, Red Moon, Big Snake--all lay silent. Oh, how everyone would miss the Snake!

At burial time, the grief over the fallen heroes reached fever pitch as the women began their wailing for the dead. The members of the tribe took comfort in the words of the Comanche who made a special effort to comfort relatives as the bodies were covered with sand. The more stern of heart took some solace in leaving the stricken Sioux lying where they had fallen for the wolves, coyotes, and birds of prey to feast upon.

Logan spent many hours concentrating on his two recent experiences with the Sioux after the tribe had returned to Bellevue.   They had taught him that the Sioux were not invincible, but that the Omaha were no match for even one of the tribes in the Sioux Nation.   Logan also was aware that two reasons the Sioux could flaunt their might were that tribes in the area were too widely separated and no one of them was strong enough to confront the Sioux by itself.   These problems were really too weighty for a boy of Logan's age, but he thought of them daily and felt certain that somehow or somewhere there was a solution.

CHAPTER FOUR

Essence of Sage and Pine

As a representative of the American Fur company, Lucien Fontenelle made his living buying furs at a low price, whether by cash or barter, and storing them in his warehouse until they could be picked up by company boats which navigated the wide Missouri. Lucien's business not only involved buying furs at the Bellevue site, but it also took him to camps of Indians, trappers and hunters, all of whom were cashing in on the lucrative beaver fur market of the time.

Each year during the very early fall, Lucien and several of his helpers would make their annual trek to the mountains in the Colorado Territory to obtain a good supply of choice mountain furs. Lucien would load down his pack horses with supplies sought by Indians and mountain men. Then, after transporting these supplies hundreds of miles through rather hostile country to selected sites, he would trade for the pelts of animals shot or trapped in the high country.

Lucien's bartering supplies usually consisted of whiskey, knives, ammunition, beads, and cloth which did not last long once they reached the trading posts along the foothills of the Rockies. Each trip to the hills was a tremendous experience for Lucien and in the years that he made these excursions, he acquired many good friends among the Indians and the rugged mountain men. Lucien felt Logan, who he hoped would one day run his business, should accompany him as soon as possible to rendezvous sites.

While in the midst of preparations for a trip to the mountains, Lucien became ill with a severe headache and diarrhea. He retired immediately upon returning home. He showed no signs of improvement the next day as he experienced chills and backache and as time went on his temperature continued to rise. Bright Sun, being an alert nurse and well experienced from her many years among the people of her tribe, soon recognized that her husband had typhus. Immediately, she moved Lucien to an isolated room and did not allow the children near him.

Through the long days that followed, Lucien's body temperature remained elevated and Bright Sun sat with him through episodes of delirium, nausea, and vomiting. She administered to Lucien's needs day and night for weeks. Lucien's temperature began to drop as the weather cooled and day by day he became stronger. Bright Sun called the children into Lucien's bedroom when it was obvious that the crisis was over and there they embraced Lucien and prayed in thanksgiving to Wakonda for sustaining him through the dreaded fever.

The business of the American Fur Company was operated by Andrew Drips in Lucien's absence. Drips was an experienced fur trader and a close friend of Lucien's for many years.

"I sorta have a feeling that you're kinda homesick for the mountains, Andrew," said Lucien to Drips as he resumed preparations for his mountain trip on his first day back at work. "How would you like to make the trip with me this time?"

"Couldn't think of anything I'd rather do," answered Andrew. "It would be like old times."

"Sorta thought I'd take John Sarpy and my son Logan as well. John is an experienced adventurer and a business head that would be an asset during the trip. Logan has proved to be quite mature in his last excursions with the Omaha. I think this trip will take the Indian affairs off his mind and teach him something about the fur business."

Lucien picked eight pack horses for the trip, each to be laden with items of barter. He chose four solid mounts for the riders and three more riding horses as spares that would carry supplies for the trading party.

Several days before the trip, Logan, Lucien, and Andrew worked on the packs that eventually would be placed on the pack horses. Among the supplies, Lucien included a large amount of ammunition and several rifles, even though he expected no serious trouble throughout the trip. In actuality, the Indians along the way usually caused no problems for men such as

Lucien who were the only sources of desired items from the eastern markets.

When the time arrived for departure, the travelers met early at the trading post, checked their mounts and pack horses, and started their long journey. For the first time on a trip away from home, Logan felt completely safe and secure. The little party was dressed warmly and the cool days and nights were delightful, particularly after an exceptionally hot summer.

The trees in the Platte valley were beginning to show some yellow, and, as the party passed onto the plains, Logan was thrilled to see massive waves of geese migrating along the river. The call of the giant birds, their white color, and their formations were an exciting experience for the young man who felt as free as one of these graceful masters of the sky.

After pushing for more than a hundred miles, the group came to a high point where they looked down on the site of the most recent encounter between the Omaha and the Sioux. Logan relived the whole incident in his mind as he scanned the distant battlefield. "We formed our defenses there in that low area and the Sioux attacked twice from that ridge above it," volunteered Logan. "Our warriors fought very bravely and some of them are buried there in the sand."

Logan noticed a strange sight as he focused in on the area where the fighting had been most intense. "Look at those death bundles on those platforms over there. There must be over twenty of them! The Sioux must have come back to give their dead a proper burial."

John, Lucien, and Andrew appreciated Logan's emotional story very much as they listened intently, and in their hearts they prayed that the Sioux had left the area for their homes to the north.

Just after breaking camp one morning and moving west along the north bank of the Platte, the party noticed that the river became very wide and swollen. It was the point where the Platte joined the Loup River from the north. As the tributary came

into view, so did a large Indian village built on the west bank
of the stream.   The village was composed mostly of earth lodge
homes that were dome-like in structure with long entrance ways.
In appearance the lodges resembled large Eskimo igloos, but were
built of huge timbers, earth, and sod. Warm in winter and cool
in summer, the lodges symbolized permanency and the non-nomadic
nature of their inhabitants.

Smoke filled the village from many fires. "This is a
village of the Pawnee," said Lucien. "There is nothing to fear
because they are friends of most white men and they probably
already know that we are here. Did you know that the first
white men to come to this area were led here by a Pawnee,
possibly to this village? I think it would be wise for us to
cross the river and say 'hello' to Buffalo Bull, the head man of
the Grand Pawnee."

The riders dipped into the shallow waters of the Loup and
rode directly across to the other side. The Pawnee could be
seen wrapped in robes and sitting atop their lodges apparently
watching some activity in the middle of the settlement. Lucien
and his party tied their horses to a corral at the edge of the
village and made their way to the center of attention. The
visitors were hardly noticed as the villagers watched half-naked
dancers in the Harvest Dance of the Maize. Many of the
villagers feasted around the fires, and despite poor visibility
through the smoke, cheering erupted occasionally as the dancers
went through their antics to the cadence of several large skin
drums placed at the edge of the clearing.

The Pawnee warriors, who generally appeared very serious and
fierce to Lucien, seemed almost jovial as the four stopped to
watch the ceremony. The trading party stood in silence for a
long time demonstrating their respect for the ceremonial dance.
Suddenly, the beat stopped, the dance ended, and the brightly
decorated dancers began mingling in the crowd. As the trading
party gazed around, they were approached by an obese and
solemn-looking Pawnee. He wore a large silver medal around his
neck and his hair was fashioned into the unique Pawnee scalp

lock.   Curious about the party's presence, the Pawnee asked, "To what do we owe this visit to the village of the Grand Pawnee?"

"We are passing through the area and we have stopped to pay our respects to Buffalo Bull, an old friend," answered Lucien.

"Chief Buffalo Bull will be very sorry that he missed your visit, but he is visiting another village of the Pawnee.   I am Slow Run, a lesser chief, and am in charge during the chief's absence.   Would you be good enough to honor me with a visit to my lodge where we can become better friends?"

Lucien accepted and Slow Run led the party to one of the typical earth lodges in the middle of the settlement.

As the visitors approached the structure, it was obvious that Slow Run had been a superior warrior in his younger years. Twelve black scalps graced his lodge pole.   The view of the inside of a Pawnee earth lodge was a new experience for Logan. He was particularly impressed by its size and how well it was built.   In the space between four large upright timbers, which served as center supports for the roof, burned a comfortable fire with the smoke exhausting up and out a large hole in the roof.   The fire and the buffalo robes on the floor around the fire were a tempting sight to the travelers who had been on the trail for several days.   The food and drink offered by Slow Run added to the pleasure of the visit.

"Lucien, you stated that you were just passing through," stated Slow Run.   "Exactly what is your mission?"

"I am a fur trader and we are on our way to the mountains to secure furs from the high country."

Slow Run indicated that the trip sounded exciting, and (even though no one invited him) that he would like very much to go along.   "Because of my responsibility to the tribe and to the aging Buffalo Bull, however, I regret that I cannot go with you," said the fat sub-chief.

To quickly change the subject, John Sarpy asked, "Why did your people treat our arrival so lightly?   What if we had been enemies?"

"My people knew of your presence on the Platte for two days," said Slow Run.   "Besides, three men and a boy represent

no threat to the Pawnee. At the moment our only threat is from
the north and the raiding Sioux.   Life right now would be very
good if only we could find a way to stop their attacks."

Logan listened very intently as Slow Run carried· out a
tirade about the Sioux.   When he finished and the conversation
continued among the adults, the same old question crossed
Logan's mind: Why is it that the Sioux are allowed to continue
their marauding, virtually unopposed, against so many different
people in so many different places?   Surely if so many people
have the same problem, why can't some way be found to stop them?

Rested during their visit with the Pawnee, the party of
traders continued its journey along the Platte.   The days were
warm and the nights cool as the travelers passed from the area
of black rich soil to the more arid hills of sand through which
the Platte wandered.   The broad, shallow river with the sandy
hills as background was indeed a beautiful and restful sight.
"Who would think that a river with no trees in its valley could
be so spectacular?" commented Lucien.   "Even the early Spaniards
who penetrated into these lands two hundred years ago must have
felt the same as we when they referred to this river as the Rio
de Jesus Maria."

Onward and westward, the party went up river.   After two
weeks on the trail, the group arrived at the confluence of the
Platte and its southern branch.   Riding toward the summit of a
hill which commands this juncture of the two rivers, they
suddenly were confronted by four Indians who had ridden to the
high point from the opposite direction.   Reaching the top before
the fur traders, the redmen sat quietly on their mounts staring
at the approaching group.   Both the ponies and the braves were
highly painted and each of the dog soldiers carried an arm
shield and a bow and arrows.   Three of the braves had feathers
tied loosely to their long black hair and one wore an impressive
buffalo cap.

"They seem wild and reckless, so let's proceed cautiously,"
said Lucien.   "John and Andrew, keep me covered with your rifles
while I ride to speak to their leader."

As Lucien rode forward with his rifle raised, the oldest of the Indians rode to meet him. The trader found that through some words and signs he could communicate with the rugged-looking brave. Lucien returned to his group following the exchange of words and gestures.

"They are Arapaho," said Lucien. "The leader has given us permission to pass because we are traders. However, he would like us to follow him to his camp which is another three miles to the west."

The warriors led and the party of traders followed closely. As they neared the village, it reflected the nomadic life-style of the tribe. More than fifty tipis composed the encampment and almost as many dogs yapped at the feet of Lucien's horses as they moved through the camp. Buffalo meat was hung everywhere drying in the southerly autumn wind. War ponies were tied near each tipi and several fires smoldered in their pits. The tight security of the camp was obvious as sentinels could be seen stationed on every hill near the village.

The braves led Lucien and the others to a central tipi from which emerged a tall, thin, young man who obviously was the leader of this particular band of Arapaho. The leader of the scouts talked with the chief and then introduced Lucien.

"Welcome to our camp," spoke the young chief as he raised his hand in a sign of peace.

"May there always be peace between us," barked Lucien as he vigorously shook the Arapaho's hand.

"You must be exhausted from the trail. Please come inside where you can refresh yourselves and where we can talk," offered the chief. The traders gratefully accepted and stepped inside the tipi.

This has to be a warring party because of the lack of women, thought Lucien as the chief passed freshly cooked buffalo and dog meats to the visitors who sat in a circle.

"We have set up this village as a base in our search for three of our women kidnapped near the Blue River," explained the chief. "It is believed that the abductors are renegades and that they fled to the South Platte. I do not believe that the Sioux are involved because they and the Arapaho have always respected each other and have been without incident for almost a hundred years."

"Whoever is responsible is now raiding into territories never before violated," added Lucien as he told of the Comanche children who had been kidnapped the previous summer.

The young chief stood after hearing Lucien's tale and with his arms raised he prayed: "Oh Great One, give us strength to overcome this transgression against our people. Ride with us as we move to recover what is ours." The traders remained silent in respect for the young man's faith, yet they couldn't help feeling the futility of his efforts and prayers.

"The day is mostly gone, Fontenelle," stated the youthful chief following his prayer. "I would consider it an honor if you and your party would stay the night with me. In the morning, however, we will leave to continue our search."

That evening by the fire, Logan pondered the unfortunate situation of the Arapaho and realized that the Omaha were not the only people facing harassment in the changing West.

The Arapaho were mostly all gone as the trading party awoke in the morning and resumed its journey up the valley of the South Platte. When certain landmarks were sighted after a few days, Lucien guided the party away from the river and into the foothills of the mountains. Following several hours of climbing, the travelers came into view of the full impact of the Rocky Mountains. Tall, snowpacked peaks in the distance made it beautifully evident that the group had almost reached its destination. Although the surrounding countryside was pleasant to the eye, the high country created an extra burden to the plainsmen who were not accustomed to the climb.

The party reached its goal after three days on the high trail--a rough frontier settlement along the Cache la Poudre River in Colorado Territory. In many respects this place with its crudely-fashioned log huts resembled Bellevue. The huts and tipis were arranged in a helter-skelter manner and there was no lane that even resembled a main street. The inhabitants of the "village" were a mixture of mountain men and Indians. At first sight, it was evident that the knife and the gun were the lawmakers of the community. In the center of the settlement stood a log hut which was longer than the rest and over its front entrance hung a battered sign of the American Fur Company. After opening the building, the traders began the task of making the place livable and unloading their pack horses. Logan built a nice fire in the crude fireplace once the tasks were finished because nights in the fall of the year were cold at this high Colorado altitude. The fur dealers positioned their bed rolls toward the rear of the trading post. This situation was by no means comfortable, but it was at least warmer than conditions they had experienced on the trail.

In the days that followed, Logan's main duty was finding food for the horses. This task took a great deal of time as he led the horses to grassy fields and watched them graze.

Anticipating that the American Fur Company representatives would be on hand, many mountain men and Indians from various neighboring tribes began to appear in camp laden with packs of beaver, elk, and muskrat pelts, seeking money, guns, cloth, knives, beads, and above all, whiskey.

The nights in the village usually resembled a misdirected jubilee. Everyone drank cheap whiskey and worked hard at being boisterous. Men danced with men to some well-exercised concertinas and mouth organs which were a part of the household goods packed by most mountain men. Most Indians joined in the festivities, but were usually wiped out early by the "booze" which flowed freely through the camp. Fights and wrestling matches many times resulted from overindulgence in this "rot-gut." Despite the ruggedness of these gatherings, few stabbings or murders occurred and even Lucien, John, and Andrew took part in the celebrating on occasion.

It was a tremendous experience for Logan to watch the bartering in the trading post as the Indians and trappers filed through. Each person was different from the others, even though all represented what one might expect from this part of the West.   Lucien had to handle every bartering case separately because each batch of furs was of different quality and size.

Some of the Utes, Cheyenne, and Arapaho were very stubborn and drove hard bargains.   None was harder to deal with than the white trapper, who not only wanted to be paid for his furs, but who also claimed compensation for his time spent in the mountains or on the prairie.   Lucien knew his values, however, and always seeming fair, managed a good profit for his company. The other members of the party learned many things about the fur trading business by watching and listening to the older professional.

Lucien's most difficult transaction came on a day when five Utes appeared in camp with several packs of weasel skins evidently trapped the winter before because of their beautiful white pelage.   At sight of them, Lucien's mind began to churn.

I've got to have those skins.   They'd sure bring a handsome price on the Saint Louis market, thought the head trader.   Their real market value is worth far more than all our money and goods.   If the Indians want that much, it would end our trip even though more beaver pelts are needed to meet company requirements, pondered Lucien.

"Five hundred dollars," offered Lucien.

"Want one thousand dollar," dickered Bad Wolf, the intelligent Ute leader.   "You know they worth thousand dollar!"

"Five hundred dollars and seven hundred dollars credit," countered Lucien.

"What is credit?" asked Bad Wolf.

Lucien attempted to explain, but with no success.

It was well known to John and Andrew that when an Indian purchased a horse or wife or anything else he considered to be a commodity, he always made full payment immediately.   So when they tried to define the term "credit" to Bad Wolf without any success, they came to realize that this form of trade was outside the comprehension of the Ute.

The deal for the ermine seemed doomed as Bad Wolf and his companions moved toward the door. Suddenly, the Ute leader noticed two Jaeger rifles that Lucien and Andrew had placed in the corner near the entrance. Both were well maintained with beautiful maple stocks.

"Five hundred dollar and two guns for all skins," grunted Bad Wolf. Knowing that the party had other rifles for the trip home and that this seemed the last chance for a deal, Lucien bellowed one word, "Sold!"

As the Utes brought in the bales of weasel skins, Lucien handed the rifles and some pouches of powder and balls to the chief. Next, he counted out five hundred dollars in currency for the Ute leader who stuffed the bills in his shirt and hurriedly left.

In Lucien's happy eyes you could tell that he had made a very good business deal. Also pleased with their good fortune, the Utes soon rode their steeds in a roll of thunder past the trading post and out of town.

Business fell off after six days on the Cache la Poudre and the party made preparations to move on. Having loaded and strapped the bulky bales of furs on the pack horses, John, Lucien, Andrew, and Logan started the second leg of their venture, this time heading north to another rendezvous on the North Platte. With the loaded horses slowing them down, the trip to the Platte was a difficult one and the plainsmen struggled hard crossing the rugged terrain.

Contrary to popular belief, crime in the early West was almost nonexistent. Even though the Indians, plainsmen, and mountain men lived hard and worked hard, they had a deep respect for private ownership and rarely did they rob each other or kill to steal another's belongings. For these reasons, most traveling parties did not take great precautions to protect themselves against highway men, but kept alert only to avoid the ravages of Indian war parties.

The Bellevue traders were no different in this regard as they rode in the direction of Fort Laramie across a large, flat, and rocky area of northern Colorado.

"Looks like a large party on the trail ahead," offered Logan, "and they're coming from the opposite direction."

It was obvious to the traders that the approaching strangers were probably highway men because their group consisted of five rugged-looking whites and three Indians, probably renegades. On closing, the strangers drew up and blocked the trail. The spokesman for the group rode forward and began a conversation with Lucien. "My name is Braxton," said the bearded but bald leader. "Who are you and who do you represent?"

"Name is Fontenelle of the American Fur Company," was the brief answer.

The hatless Braxton, whose weather-beaten face showed him to be a man of much outdoor exposure, moved his coat exposing two large pistols. The rest of his group moved up to positions at Braxton's side. Braxton continued his query: "Bet that's a rich load yer packin' on them horses?"

"Elk and beaver hides from the Poudre area," Lucien answered cautiously, sizing up the helpless position his group was in.

"Hate to see that young boy get hurt," replied Braxton. "What do you say if we tax you half the load to cross these lands that belong to me? There will then be no trouble."

"These lands probably belong to the Arapaho or the Cheyenne and even they would allow us free passage," was Lucien's quick retort as he racked his brain for a way out of a bad situation. Nothing he thought of seemed to be the right solution and he felt that even if he gave the bandits the whole of his possessions, they probably would kill everyone anyway.

Just as Lucien was about to offer half of his furs to the bandits, Braxton dismounted and walked over and looked at Logan. "One of you must be a squaw man!" he roared. He then walked back to his horse, rose to his saddle, and muttered, "Oh well, he's just another rotten, stinkin' . . ."

The area rocked with a shattering crack and Braxton and three of his henchmen lay dead at the feet of their horses with huge bullet holes in their chests. Witnessing this sudden change of events, the rest of the bandits swung their horses around and fled into the moor to the east.

The trading party turned to the direction from which the shots had come. While still stunned, they viewed four rugged frontiersmen standing on the top of a huge boulder retamping their muzzle loaders. Lucien wanted to ride forward to thank the foursome, but was too limp even to do that. He merely climbed off his mount, leaned against it and waited for the rescuers to join him.

The riflemen approached and they were completely unfamiliar to the Bellevue group. John Sarpy was the first to extend his hand to the men who somewhat resembled one another because of their bronzed faces, grubby wide-brimmed hats and buckskin clothes, leggings, and moccasins.

"Well, we actually got that scavenger Braxton," said one of the four. "My name is Mattox and this is Wulff, Steffen, and Briggs."

Lucien introduced his party and heartily thanked the four for their help. He then asked them if there was anything he could do to help them. "We don't need transportation if we take Braxton's horses, but we sure could use some grub. We've been livin' on nothin' but water for the last three days," said Mattox.

Lucien then decided to make camp and feed the weak and very deserving riflemen. As the Bellevue party unloaded the horses and prepared a camp, Mattox explained how they had been robbed three days before by Braxton's group and how the bandits had killed a member of their band who objected to the robbery.

"Braxton made one mistake and that was to leave us our rifles," Mattox stated. "We knew that if we waited here on this trail long enough, we'd get help. We didn't dream that Braxton would have the gall to come back this way."

The mountain men lounged like monarchs while the traders waited on them hand and foot. After a good meal, Mattox and his partners rounded up the horses of the four dead men and found a packet of money on Braxton which more than compensated them for their earlier losses. The four bodies were buried in a common pit. During the burial no one mentioned any last words, nor was silence observed as dirt was tossed on the stiff corpses. To Logan, the whole incident seemed ironic, that here in the land of the Indian, white men were still a threat to one another.

On the morning of the next day, as the Bellevue traders prepared their mounts and pack horses, they were approached by Mattox. "Since we have no supplies and grub to continue our trapping operation," he noted, "would you mind if we rode along with you to Fort Laramie? We'd be happy to pay for our keep."

"After what you've done for us, I'd be happy to grubstake you for as long as you'd care to tag along," Lucien offered. "Maybe you'd like to come back to Bellevue and go to work for the fur company?"

"No thanks," barked Mattox. "We'll just bother you as far as the fort and then we'll be off to the high country. Those hills become part of your soul and you just can't leave 'em, not even for the comforts the likes of Bellevue."

The familiar stockade forts that were erected at strategic points in the West in the early 1800's were constructed for several reasons. These strong-holds, with their trained garrisons, were actual anchors in a chain of determination of the U.S. government to secure and hold newly acquired property against foreign invasion. The forts also served in a weak attempt to maintain peace between the white opportunists and the Indians and at times the forts even served to maintain peace between the many warring tribes of the plains and mountains. In these early days, the forts in the territory attracted merchants and customers alike. Many times individual Indians would set up permanent residences near a fort instead of venturing about with their respective tribes. Under the protection of the stockade and its troopers, they formed a society all their own. Occasionally, whole tribes would camp near the forts, tending to add to the interest and color of these western "cities."

Stockade Solitaire

You rule by your presence,
boiling pot of the plain.
Some comfort in your essence,
others look with disdain.

Sometimes from the population of these centers of activity, and Fort Laramie was no exception, would emerge the individualist who stood out from the ordinary citizen of the fort.   One such character was an old Cheyenne brave named Watoga, who long before the fall of 1837 had been left behind by his nomadic people.

Watoga lived in a very tall impressive tipi near the east wall of the Laramie fort.   The old brave's bronze face was carved with deep vertical lines and his head was capped with heavy grey hair which hung loose and uncombed about his stooped shoulders.   Draped about his degenerating body was an old fading buffalo robe that bore the paintings of his many wars, coups, and hunts which once had brought him fame, now forgotten.   From beneath the robe protruded two spindly legs, heavily bowed from his long years on horseback.   Watoga's feet were adorned with beautifully beaded moccasins which were indicative of his station in life--a retired, leisurely old bull whose only activity was that of drinking, celebrating his long dangerous life, and passing out advice.

On one of his daily rounds, Watoga was the lone figure on the trail as Lucien and his party approached the fort. Identifying Lucien, the old man produced a broad smile exposing two teeth, the only ones left in his mouth.   Lucien couldn't help recognizing the picturesque old warrior who stood as proud as he did when he was the most decorated brave in all the camps of the Cheyenne.

"Loochan," cried the old man.   "You have finally come back to see your old friend.   Let's go to tipi, get drunk, and raise hell!"

Lucien was all smiles as he climbed down from his horse and hugged Watoga.   "I can't get drunk with you anymore," said Lucien.   "You see I've brought my son so I must stick strictly to business."

John, Logan, Andrew, and the others couldn't believe what they were seeing as Lucien grasped the old man by the hand and led him around the horses to introduce him to everyone.

Standing before Logan, the old Indian analyzed the young man's face and body. In true Cheyenne custom, he issued his approval with these words: "Brave one, your mother must be of excellent stock to give you those alert eyes and strong facial features. Your physique and strength are no mystery to me because you resemble your father when he and I hunted in the hills many years ago. Alleluia, another Loochan Fontenelle with the face of a savage!"

In the days that followed, the trading party occupied the quarters owned by the fur company within the fort. Here business flourished and many excellent furs were obtained. Logan idled away his time inside the fort speaking with the soldiers, watching the troopers drill, and listening to the stories of the Indians, trappers, mountainmen, and plainsmen that frequented the trading post. Logan also spent many hours with Watoga, who was delighted in having someone who would take time to listen to his tales of the past.

Logan did not feel, however, that his time was wasted because by listening to the old man, he absorbed much about the customs, beliefs, and activities of the Cheyenne, Arapaho, and most of all, the Sioux. Logan learned from the old-timer that the Cheyenne did live somewhat in harmony with the various tribes of the plains mostly because they were strong, brave, and willing to fight for their rights and land claims. This he felt was a valuable lesson.

One day Watoga approached Lucien and Logan with an exciting proposition. "I have just heard that a large portion of the Cheyenne is camped about ten miles east of here. I am very eager to visit with my people and I wonder if Logan would like to go with me. It would be a tremendous experience for him."

"How do you feel about visiting the Cheyenne, Logan?" asked Lucien who had spent many days with the Cheyenne himself.

"It would be a great thrill and I would be safe with Watoga," answered Logan.

With permission granted, Watoga took Logan off to see the "Human Beings," a then-common name used by the Cheyenne.

The camp of the Cheyenne was an impressive sight from the distant hills. Its tipis were numerous, tall, and colorful. All aspects of the village were indicative of a proud people. As Logan watched Watoga, he could see the old man change with every step nearer the camp. A stooped, greying, wrinkled cast-off suddenly bore the image of an experienced, bold warrior complete with straight back, broad shoulders and protruding chin. Logan mused that this was a fleeting transfiguration of an old man reliving his youthful days when he rode at the head of the Cheyenne hordes that once ruled the western Nebraska plains.

As the proud old man and the boy reached the Cheyenne tipis, dogs began barking at the feet of their mounts. Unswayed and looking straight ahead, Watoga marched his pony past peering women and children, past a large collection of war horses, through the ranks of a large gathering of Cheyenne warriors, and into chief's country, which was marked by a ring of lodge poles from which hung souvenirs of great hunts and warring campaigns of this Cheyenne division. Logan was all eyes and ears as he trailed the brazen Watoga, who even though an intruder, was obviously Cheyenne. The old brave's horse no more than passed the first lodge poles, from which hung several scalps, an axe, and a bison skull, when a young chief halted him inquiring about his presence.

The questions had no more than left the young man's lips when Watoga bombarded him verbally. "Out of my way, dust of the prairie," he growled, "before I grind you into the earth. I am here to see Stone Face. Go tell him that the warrior Watoga now graces his camp and that he must see him immediately." At those words the impressed young man hurried to the chief's tipi. Watoga remained where he had been halted, sitting high and proud upon his black steed.

Stone Face was stunned as he went to the entrance of his tipi and viewed the sight of the proud old brave on his horse with the contrasting Indian boy halted some distance behind.

Out of total respect for Watoga's reputation, the chief proceeded to walk the distance between his lodge and the old man. To Watoga this was the act of a humble yet great man, so to respond properly he dismounted and walked to greet the chief in open field.

"I am proud to warrant a visit from the great Watoga," remarked the chief as he embraced the old Cheyenne. "You must be exhausted from your trip, so come to my tipi for refreshments."

Watoga motioned for Logan to come forward and as the boy rode up, Stone Face extended his hand.   "This is Logan of the Omaha," offered Watoga and Logan basked in the fact that the old but respected man was his friend.

Inside the tipi there was great jubilation as the chief and Watoga compared stories of events of the great past of the Cheyenne.   The chief's wife and daughter waited on their needs while Logan remained quiet, soaking up every bit of information that was passed between the great leaders past and present.

Eventually Stone Face turned to Logan. "So you are Omaha?" asked the chief. "I thought the Omaha had been annihilated long ago by an enemy along the Big Sioux River."

Logan's answer was sharp and carried a clear message. "My people have survived the massacre that was carried out by the Santee Sioux," he stated. We, the Omaha, now exist as a barb in the side of all the Sioux and we will soon challenge them along the Missouri and the Platte. Only last summer near the Platte we soaked the sand red with Sioux blood."

Watoga smiled and Stone Face sat back wide-eyed upon hearing these words. The chief was utterly astounded that these words should come from this quiet, well-mannered lad.

"I like you boy," Stone Face declared. "You sound more like a Cheyenne brave than a young man raised along the quiet Missouri. If what you say is true about the Omaha, I do not want them as our enemy. So, I would like to pledge a spirit of cooperation between our people--one that will last long past the time when my bones and Watoga's are dust." Stone Face then lit up a long, beautiful, red stone pipe and passed it to Logan to smoke as a symbol of alliance.

"I smoke for my grandfather, Big Elk, great chief of the Omaha," said Logan, "for I know that this would be his wish." The brief ceremony pleased Watoga because he knew that this was no doubt the first time a pact of this magnitude was sealed between two great tribes with someone as youthful as Logan doing the honors.

"I would appreciate it if the two of you would stay with me during your visit," offered Stone Face. "In a day or so a contingent of Arapaho will arrive here and following that we expect a portion of the Comanche tribe to rendezvous with us. The purpose of this gathering is to discuss how to recover five Comanche children and three Arapaho women recently kidnapped by renegades."

Logan then related the story of how the Omaha had befriended a young band of Comanche in search of the five children and how this band had later aided in driving off attacking Sioux.

Watoga and Logan accepted Stone Face's invitation and took up quarters in an empty tipi close to that of the chief. At approximately noon of the next day, the Cheyenne received word that the Arapaho were approaching their village from the south. The Cheyenne were not moved with any great anticipation because the Cheyenne and Arapaho were very friendly with each other and meetings of the tribes were commonplace. Nevertheless, upon receipt of word of the arrival, Stone Face mustered his braves and rode out to meet the rather large force led by an older chief named Lone Fire, a man respected for his great wisdom and bravery. As the Arapaho approached, Stone Face lined up his men abreast of each other as if to review the Arapaho when they passed by.

Mounted next to the Cheyenne chief, Logan felt a part of the Cheyenne warrior force. To Logan, the Cheyenne appeared young, sleek, and strong. The Arapaho seemed more confident and war-weathered and commanded respect from their appearance alone. It was a great moment for Logan--one about which a young man dreams.

Adding to the excitement of the meeting of the two great tribes, several large drums began to beat out a slow tempo in the Cheyenne camp, designating that all was well with the visit by the Arapaho.

Logan and Watoga wandered through the Cheyenne village as the Arapaho set up camp nearby. They finally wandered into the chief's enclave and relaxed in their assigned tipi. As the two continued in conversation through the afternoon, Watoga appeared curious about the Comanche. The old warrior was reluctant to tell Logan, but finally admitted that in all of his campaigns and wanderings he never had encountered the Comanche. This placed Logan in a unique position where he could finally tell something to the famous Cheyenne and have him listen with full attention.

It was early next morning when word was received from the scouts that the Comanche were approaching the Cheyenne-Arapaho camp. Emotion ran high through the large encampment for this was the first formal meeting of these tribes. Adorned in their most colorful dress, the warriors of the combined forces under their respective leaders mounted and rode to salute the horsemen with the great reputation. Both forces left very hurriedly. Logan and Watoga, however, straggled in their efforts to witness the Comanche meeting.

The old brave and Logan did not catch up with the merged tribes until they had drawn up on a high promontory to await the Comanche horde whose near presence was obvious from an approaching column of dust that could be seen rising just beyond the nearby hills.

Taking his usual liberties, Watoga moved to the most prominent point of review where the two chiefs waited in full dress. He was not rebuked by either chief and even Logan's presence in the forward position was approved by a smile from Lone Fire.

All was still as the combined forces waited. Suddenly, like a tornado breaking from the southwest, a roar could be heard from beyond the closest hill. Before another minute passed, the hilltop was covered with hundreds of scantily dressed Comanche. They paused momentarily to view the waiting tribes; then on one command, they swooped down the long sandhill with the speed of antelope and the grace of hawks. As the Comanche rode past the reviewing position of the chiefs, the skill of the horsemen was awesome, bringing salutes and cheers from the ranks of the Cheyenne and Arapaho. As the riders swept by, Watoga and the chiefs were shocked to see a Comanche break ranks and ride directly toward them. Logan too was amazed as he identified the young chief, Light Horse, his friend, who apparently had recognized him in his forward position with the chiefs. Light Horse reined up in front of Logan, saluted him with raised rifle and asked, "Will White Horse ride with Light Horse and the Comanche?"

Logan smiled and walked his horse forward to join the young Comanche.

On signal from Light Horse, both the young Omaha and the Comanche chieftain rode quickly to join the last of the braves who were rushing in.

In all of his many years, Watoga had seen few things that surprised him more. In awe, he sat on his horse with his mouth gaping while pointing at the riders as they moved on in the distance.

It was high noon when the main chiefs of the three tribes met in council. Stone Face, Lone Fire, and the Comanche, Spanish Man, all in colorful full dress assembled in chief's country of the Cheyenne camp with their warriors looking on. The mood appeared to be one of great friendship, for all three tribes had a common goal.

Spanish Man stood as the others sat. Casting an air of great dignity, he addressed the throng: "My Cheyenne and Arapaho brothers, it has been many, many years since there has been any conflict among us. In the distant past, in wars between the tribes, warriors took the lives of warriors, but never did innocent and helpless people suffer. We practiced a code of honor in those conflicts. In recent times, however, it appears that the codes of the past are no longer respected by wandering renegades. Already children have been taken from us and women from the Arapaho. Soon people of the Cheyenne will be subjected to this same fate. The warriors here today represent a strong force that should not tolerate these practices. The Comanche and I believe that we should seek payment for past offenses in blood and scalps!" On hearing these words, the congregation of warriors stood and responded in a single war yell that shook the surrounding valley.

Stone Face stood next and spoke but a few words: "The Cheyenne agree that the acts of our enemies must be revenged. Let us all allow the Comanche to rest and regain their strength and then let us move as one against the enemy." Again the valley rocked with the loud approval of the onlooking composite of braves.

As the reverberations of the war whoops died in the distant hills, a hush fell over the bronzed warriors. Lone Fire, the revered war chief of the Arapaho stood in front of the fighting horde. "It is apparent that my Comanche and Cheyenne brothers are one of mind, for their words are short," uttered the Arapaho chief. "I will not speak long either, but I do want to say that we must be thorough when we teach the enemy their lesson. Let it be an unforgettable one!"

As Lone Fire sat down, the war yells burst forth for a third time and before the chiefs could retire to the lodge of Stone Face for more talks, the braves of the three tribes worked themselves into a frenzy. Arapaho danced with Comanche and Comanche with Cheyenne. It was an event never seen before on the plains and the enthusiasm lasted until most of the warriors collapsed from exhaustion.

At sunrise on the next day, everything was in disarray from the spirited war dance the night before. Horses, weapons, and braves were scattered everywhere. Only the chiefs, Watoga, and Logan had the presence of mind to retire to their proper lodgings--the chiefs for reasons of dignity; Logan for reasons of youth; and Watoga for reasons of age.

A full day was spent putting things together for the campaign to the north. Even though desire was strong in the hearts of both Watoga and Logan to accompany the war party, Logan knew that he must return to the fort and to Lucien. Watoga knew that a venture of this magnitude was only for the young and sturdy. Consequently, the old man and Logan spent the day saying farewell to new and old friends among the massive battle group.

On the next day, as the warriors pulled out of camp in spirited fashion, Logan and Watoga mounted their own horses, but faced them in a different direction. Neither of the two looked back until they reached the peak of a prominent hill to the west. Sneaking a brief glimpse from there, Watoga could see the dust of the long column of warriors heading northward. Then, as the pair continued toward the fort, Logan recognized tears in the eyes of the old man. In no way did Logan consider this as a sign of weakness because he fully understood the feelings of the bent grey figure whose spirit had outlasted his body and who uniquely had lived long enough to witness himself as a Cheyenne legend.

CHAPTER FIVE

Mormon Hollow

In 1839, Florissant, Missouri, a hamlet outside of Saint Louis was home of the Jesuit order in its Saint Louis Province. It was a seat of higher learning and a land of large vineyards and wineries that were the main source of support for the institution. These quiet acres, besides being an academic oasis, was the launching point for Jesuit missionaries carrying Christian doctrine to the heathen West. Pierre DeSmet, the Blackrobe, used Florissant as his base of operations and retreat, so naturally it was this school that he felt was well-suited for the sons of Lucien Fontenelle.

In the spring of the year, Father DeSmet again paid a visit to the Fontenelle home en route to Florissant. After a few days, he left in the company of Logan and Albert. The trip to Saint Louis on board one of the steamboats of the American Fur Company was indeed a great experience for the boys, as was the hustling city of Saint Louis.

The boys from the frontier fit in very well at the Jesuit secondary school, which was taught primarily by seminary scholastics, not only because of their intelligence, but because of their athletic prowess and their firsthand knowledge of the raw West. At times in session with their schoolmates, the thrilling stories related by Logan seemed to exceed even those of Father DeSmet.

For two years the boys grew both academically and physically at the school. Albert excelled in mathematics and the basic sciences, while Logan did best in languages and philosophy. On occasion the boys wrote messages to their family and friends at Bellevue. Sometimes, too, they received letters telling of the latest developments at home.

As the boys were entering their third year of training, with each seriously considering a missionary career, the word arrived that Lucien was very ill again with typhoid fever. To the disappointment of all the teachers and their classmates, Logan and Albert hurriedly packed and made their way to Saint Louis to catch the next steamboat up the Missouri. The boys were obliged to make the trip without escort because DeSmet was away from Florissant at the time. They arrived at Bellevue too late to see their father alive. Lucien had died four days before their landing and had been laid to rest at his favorite place high in the wooded hills overlooking the river.

The homecoming was a very comforting occasion for Bright Sun, who had struggled through Lucien's illness as she had in his first episode, only to lose in the endeavor. In the days following the boy's arrival, things were very melancholy as the memories of Lucien lingered on. Just as always, though, time healed this very large wound.

One thing that did not heal after the passing of Lucien, however, was the fur trading business. After the loss of Lucien's leadership, the enterprise in the area seemed to succumb slowly to financial failure. Many felt that a shortage of beaver in the mountains actually brought on the demise of the industry, yet others felt that the lack of a man of vision and foresight at the top was the main reason for its collapse. Regardless, shortly following Lucien's death, Bright Sun sold the business to Andrew Drips.

Early in the summer of 1841, Drips organized a rather large trip to Fort Laramie and the mountains. One of the first persons to sign up for the journey was Kit Carson who for the past years had been living with the Omaha and raising a family with Moneta. As the traders embarked on their trip, Moneta, the Fontenelles, the Bellevue community, and perhaps Carson himself did not know that Carson would never return. As history would demonstrate, Carson was to go on to a very famous and active life in other areas of the West. Moneta was never to see him again and Logan and Iron Eye but one more time.

In the absence of Lucien, the Indian influence became stronger in the Fontenelle family because of the leanings of Bright Sun. Logan and Albert, even though they had more formal education than most in the area, took to the ways of the Omaha tribe with the guidance and support of their grandfather, Big Elk.   Logan and Iron Eye, his cousin, became even closer and as the months passed they grew in stature and experience as part of the warrior force of the tribe.

Andrew Drips became the bearer of bad news on the day of the return of the trading party from Fort Laramie.   First, Drips reported to Moneta that Kit had left the trading post at Laramie and was last seen heading in a southerly direction with no apparent intention of returning to Bellevue.   Secondly, Drips relayed a message to Logan from the Cheyenne, Watoga, that the probe by the three tribes in search of kidnapped women and children had ended in failure.   Apparently no contact had been made with renegade parties, hence nothing had been resolved concerning the grievances of the Arapaho, Cheyenne, and Comanche.

Logan showed no emotion when he heard the news about Carson because he felt that Kit was a good man and would look after his family.   However, when Drips delivered the message about the failure of the expedition, the response from Logan would have curled the ears of his former Jesuit mentors.   It was obvious to Logan and others present that he was not the missionary type; he was not a DeSmet.   At this moment he felt only hatred and wanted only revenge for the Comanche and Arapaho.   He was a Watoga of old, an avenger, a collector of scalps.

Of the many things written about the Omaha tribe, what has not been emphasized was the great heart and kindness that composed these hardy people.   Even though fierce and absolute in battle, they continually demonstrated generosity for their friends and compassion for the weak and helpless.   Of all the single individuals and groups of people who passed through Omaha lands on their way west and who were befriended and assisted by this ravaged tribe, few if any, thanked them, acknowledged their help, or attempted to repay them once they had attained their goals.

Eventually, the remnants of a once proud and respected people would endure in poverty in northeastern Nebraska.   Yet rich and influential descendants of thousands of white migrants, who survived in their journeys west only because of the charity of the Omaha, would remain apathetic to their condition.

It was late in the year of 1846 when Omaha Indian scouts sighted a wagon train on the east bank of the Missouri River opposite Bellevue. Logan, who was twenty-one years old and an important figure in the tribe, was sent by Big Elk to investigate the train.

"Go to the east bank of the river, Logan, and learn what you can about those people and their future plans," requested Big Elk. "I can't understand who would be migrating this late in the year."

Swimming the river on his new steed, Logan found a motley caravan. These people look like fugitives, thought Logan. It was obvious to him that the train had been put together in a hurry from the lack of provisions and equipment. Groping through the unorganized settlers, Logan found the leader—a tall, impressive man named Brigham Young.

"We are a vanguard of Mormons fleeing religious persecution in Nauvoo, Illinois," Young told Logan. "I have been hoping that we could find a winter campsite here along the Missouri because it's too late to move any further west."

"The high bluffs on the west bank would be the best winter campsite in this whole area," said Logan to Young. "Big Elk, my chief, will have to give the permission for you to move there, however."

Seeing the adverse conditions of the women and children and the caravan as a whole, Logan couldn't help equating these people to the migrating Omaha when they first came to the valley many, many years before. With these thoughts urging him on, Logan hurried across the river to talk to Big Elk about allowing these wretched people on Omaha lands.

Hearing of the plight of the Mormons, Big Elk's first reaction was to help, but as he analyzed the magnitude of the task, he had second thoughts. Where would he house the number of people standing across the river? How would he feed them?

The lodges and tipis in the village were already filled and the food supply scarcely would last the tribe until early spring. The great chief had indeed found himself in the worst dilemma of his long leadership of the tribe.

"Contact the Mormon leader and invite his people to the west side of the river," ordered the chief with complete disregard for the problems that seemed to lie ahead. "Also show them the best place to ford the river and where to set up winter camp."

Every make and type of wagon imaginable rumbled across the river at the ford pulled by oxen, mules, horses, and even humans. It was an incredible sight for Logan. He viewed the variety of human beings packed in the train as the wagons filed past him. The young, very young, middle-aged, and old did not appear to be adequately clothed to face the elements of the prairie, nor did they appear adequately equipped for the ordeal. Each wagon was crammed with goods and belongings, little of which seemed useful for survival in this raw country.

Logan took his place at the head of the wagons following the crossing and after riding about a mile, he called a halt at the entrance of a long, narrow, deep ravine nestled in the hills and bluffs that paralleled the river.

"This hollow has good timber and is supplied with plenty of good water from several springs," Logan told the Mormon leader.

"The Lord has truly blessed us to lead us to this bountiful site," Young responded. "You are truly an answer to all our prayers."

Young directed his people to occupy the hollow and at once the industrious Mormons began the task of building cabins. The steep sides of the glen also provided excellent sites for those who decided to build dug-outs for even better winter shelter.

It was a balmy Sunday afternoon in the middle of October when Big Elk led about a hundred of his people to the Mormon camp. The hardworking Mormons were taken completely by surprise as the Omaha filed into the hollow. The appearance of the fierce-looking warriors utterly shocked some of the whites who never had seen Indian braves before. Many novices to the ways of the West even picked up weapons and pointed them at the mounted tribal members which included women and children as well as braves. The Omaha never lost their control and composure despite this show of ignorance.

Big Elk stopped his painted steed and dismounted when the column was well into the hollow. Learning of the arrival of the Omaha, Brigham Young hurried to greet Big Elk who was introduced by Logan. As the leaders were making their salutations, the Mormons gathered about them and many took seats on one of the steep slopes of the glen. When all had calmed down, Brigham stood facing his people and spoke: "Good friends, I would like to introduce Big Elk, chief of the Omaha, through whose generosity we have been allowed to occupy this ideal site. The chief has some words that he would like to present to us and I would appreciate it if you would give him your complete attention."

Big Elk didn't really need Young's plea for attention. Big Elk presented an air of dignity and garnered all the respect needed as the tall, greying chief stood to speak dressed in his long robe. His eloquent tongue held the Mormons in awe because the last thing they expected to hear in the wilderness was a "savage" with full command of the English language.

"Christian friends," the host leader spoke invitingly, "I have come here to welcome you to Omaha lands. We, the Omaha, are well aware that you have been torn from your homes and forced to the trail with no plans or provisions. We also are aware of how severe winters can take their toll in this area. I am sorry that our tribe does not have the lodges to house you, but as of today half of our braves will work with you in building shelters. The rest of my braves will leave tomorrow for the Elkhorn River valley to hunt deer and antelope for your food coffers. As the winter progresses, we will share with you our supply of maize, some of which you will find now on the backs of our pack horses. Use it wisely. I am certain that with the help of Wakonda, we will survive the winter and avoid the pangs of hunger. Remember, we the Omaha are your friends."

As Big Elk finished, Young again stood in front of his people saying: "I would like you now to go to your knees so that we can pray. Almighty Lord, we indeed have many things to be happy about today and we want to thank you for your guidance and help here in the wilderness. We thank you for the presence of the Omaha in our hour of greatest need. Dear Lord, grant our people deliverance in the trials ahead so that we may carry your word to the place you have chosen for us."

The Omaha filed out of the hollow during Young's prayer leaving the Mormons with the knowledge that in the West help and friendship can be experienced in many strange ways.

Logan stared at the fire that night in the quiet of his warm, snug home and his only thoughts were of the Mormons in their camp. Were they warm? Were they hungry? He could find solace only in the fact that he and the Omaha had done all that was humanly possible to add to the comfort of the immigrants. In deep meditation, he made a silent pledge to help much more if possible.

As the autumn days passed, not only did the Omaha work hard to feed and shelter the Mormons, but they set an example for the white occupants of Bellevue. The trappers, drunks, missionaries, hunters, loafers, all of whom were men of great experience, found more meaning to their lives as they pitched in to help the efforts in the hollow. What was Nauvoo's loss was a remarkable addition to the history of events that still haunt the silent, steep hills that stand as sentinels along the wide Missouri.

With the help of the people in the area, it wasn't long before the hollow was transformed into an adequate home for the Latter Day Saints. Life had settled down considerably until one chilly morning in November, when another large contingent of Mormons appeared on the east bank of the river. Hurriedly, Brigham Young crossed to meet them.

Young explained the situation to the head of the new arrivals: "Our friends are now secure in a warm glen across the river, thanks to the help and generosity of the Omaha Indians

who live there. We cannot impose on them more. I will arrange
for us to cross the river and then we will proceed north to a
good site for another winter camp."

Young negotiated with John Sarpy to shuttle the second
contingent across the river on a crudely built ferry constructed
by the Bellevue businessman because the river was higher than
when the first Mormons had forded it. Once the new arrivals had
safely crossed, Young led them to the other site later known as
Florence, Nebraska. Since the second group of Mormons had not
left Illinois as hurriedly as the first group, it was better
equipped for construction and a large camp was constructed at
Florence during November and December as the weather permitted.

The harsh winter of 1846 proved that the Mormons were
novices to the ways and elements of the West and only a hardy
people with a dedicated cause could have survived the conditions
that existed. Of the thousands of Mormons in the two camps, no
one died in Mormon Hollow that winter, but some seventy souls
passed away in the north camp for various reasons such as
exposure, pneumonia, small pox, typhoid, and old age. The
people buried in a plot of ground to the west of the north camp
were placed in very shallow graves. So shallow are the
interments at Mormon Cemetery, Florence, Nebraska, that the
caretakers of the gardens on these premises today uncover the
bones of the early immigrants merely by hoeing weeds from around
the flowers.

> The voice comes screaming from the deep
> and hallowed, shallow ground:
> "Preserve the land that we have won.
> Do not lose it while you sleep."

Logan, tall and bronzed from his Indian and French
heritages, stood silently on a high promontory overlooking the
busy and smoky camp of the Saints. Many thoughts ran through
his mind as he pondered the future of the vulnerable people
below. He envisaged their pending trek west and wondered how
they might withstand a Sioux attack as they moved through the
vastness of Nebraska Territory. Would they endure? Would they

reach the area they believed to be the "promised land," where they would be free to worship and grow in their own way?

A rugged individualist in his own right, Logan thoroughly respected the Mormon independence and philosophy, but he realized that all the independence and strong attitude in the Mormon camp could not deliver them through the Sioux raiding parties in the grasslands to the west. As Logan meditated on the seriousness of the situation, he had a renewal of his earlier thoughts of the need for organization of the tribes against the Sioux threat.

Logan was well aware that many white immigrants leaving Saint Joseph on their way to the Oregon Territory were relatively successful in reaching their goal. He believed that their success was due to the fact that the route of the Oregon migrators did not pass through Sioux lands. Once they left Saint Joseph, they traversed districts of the friendly Kansa and indifferent Kiowa. Upon reaching the Platte, they had only to contend with the Pawnee. At the junction of the South Platte, they came under the curious eyes of the Arapaho and Cheyenne who by this time were used to the traffic of the white man to the west. How much more fortunate to ride the Oregon Trail than to travel, as the Mormons were planning, through the territory of the dreaded Sioux.

Logan spent many hours worrying about how the Mormons would gain safe passage along that portion of the Platte River where the Sioux were a threat. He knew that Big Elk would permit Omaha braves to escort the travelers through some of the land in question. He also knew that if the Sioux learned of the Mormon migration beforehand, they could be waiting in force to ambush the settlers. In such a case, the strength of the Omaha would be greatly inadequate. At all cost, any preparations for the Mormon trip had to be kept in complete secrecy. Also, it was imperative that assistance be recruited in escorting the migrants across the hostile lands.

In his planning to attempt to make conditions safer for the westward movement of the Mormons, Logan thought of the Pawnee and his father's friend, Buffalo Bull, of the Grand Pawnee.

Could the chief be convinced to come to the assistance of the white migrators?

Seeking aid in his thinking, Logan rode to the Omaha encampment to discuss his ideas with Big Elk and Iron Eye.

"It is a good idea to try to get the Pawnee to help," said Iron Eye, "but it will take some selling. I suggest you see what Big Elk thinks."

As always, Big Elk was understanding and helpful while Logan outlined his plan before a warm fire in the chief's lodge.

"If you approach Buffalo Bull with this idea, you will have to be well prepared, cautious, and diplomatic," said the chief. "Even though friendly, Buffalo Bull and the Pawnee are not like the Omaha, Ponca, or Osage. They are not idealistic and believe in acting only for a profit or some advantage. If you are going to convince the old warrior to afford protection for the Mormons, you will have to convince him that it will be of some advantage to the Pawnee. Rest assured he will drive a hard bargain."

Logan and Iron Eye left the lodge of the Omaha chief with his words still ringing in their ears. Logan could think of no reason why the Pawnee should concern themselves with the welfare of the Mormons. On the way back to Bellevue, Logan searched the depths of his mind for a convincing point to use on the cagey, old chief of the major populace along the Platte. Many cold days passed as Logan contemplated his dilemma. In the final analysis, he decided he had no good sales talk. However, Logan made up his mind to visit Buffalo Bull and call upon his humane nature to agree to protect the Mormons.

Packed and equipped for the trail, Iron Eye and Logan rode west one morning in early March. By this time in their lives, the route along the Platte was quite familiar to them, but each time they had followed this route, it had meant new adventures and experiences. The two braves covered many miles by day, but at night they had to endure the cold with only their buffalo robes or make-shift shelters to protect them. It was a frigid trip, and the only warm feeling they had along the way was from the sight of the Pawnee earth lodges at the mouth of the Loup River.

The grim-looking Pawnee in their long robes sat silently atop their lodges as the young Omaha entered the massive village. The Pawnee always appeared unrelenting to Logan because of their reserved, unexcitable personalities and this made him very nervous in the role of an ambassador seeking favors.

Logan recognized the lodge of Buffalo Bull from his previous visit. As the young men approached the dwelling, their path was quickly blocked by two tall, fierce-looking braves who held the visitor's ponies and demanded that they dismount.

"I am Logan Fontenelle, son of Lucien Fontenelle," spoke Logan. "I have come to speak to the great Buffalo Bull." Even though silent, one of the Pawnee appeared to comprehend what Logan was saying. He motioned for the pair to follow him while the other brave led the horses to the tying area. Once in front of the chief's lodge, the trio halted and the Pawnee brave stepped inside. Emerging soon, the escort ushered the Omaha inside.

"The two of you are indeed welcome to the warmth of my fire," said the tall, greying chief. "Which of you is the son of Fontenelle?"

"I am the son of Lucien," stated Logan humbly.

"I was saddened when I learned of your father's death," offered Buffalo Bull as he embraced the young Fontenelle. "Lucien was a brave and kind friend and I will miss him as I would one of my own sons in death. I hope that you young men have learned well from him and have the heart to carry on in his great example."

Buffalo Bull offered the young men some comfortable seats and food and drink after his unusual expression of sentiment. While enjoying their refreshments, Logan explained to the old chief that he had a matter of great importance to discuss. Buffalo Bull suggested, however, that because it was late in the day, the two should occupy the guest lodge next door, rest, and talk of important matters the next day.   The Omaha braves welcomed this suggestion because they were exhausted from the cold days on the trail.   Upon looking after their horses, Logan and Iron Eye each fell into a deep sleep, assured of their security within the friendly village.

Late in the morning of the next day, Logan and his partner were awakened by several Pawnee women laden with food.   This was a banquet compared to what they had been forced to eat along the Platte.   Toward the end of the meal, a stern-looking Buffalo Bull stood in the doorway of the lodge.

"I've come to speak of important matters," said the chief as he moved to the fire.   "It is a real diversion to have you young men visit us and to think of things other than war, war, war."

"What war problems do you have?" inquired Iron Eye.

"The Sioux!" responded Buffalo Bull.   "They have been everywhere this winter raiding our people on the Platte and up the Loup.   One young Oglala, Sharp Horn, has been particularly devastating.   He is the nephew of Goes To War and is more of a tactician than his uncle.   He fights every battle as if he were the defender, fighting for his life, rather than the aggressor.   I do not understand this increased activity of the Sioux.   I have never seen it like this before."

With the veins standing high in his neck and anger in his eyes, Logan added, "Sharp Horn is an aggressive fanatic.   We should have killed him years ago when we caught him stealing horses near Bellevue."

Logan realized that while the Sioux raids were still on the mind of Buffalo Bull, this probably was the time to make his point about the Mormons.   He broached the purpose of their call: "In a few weeks a helpless wagon train of whites will be heading west from the Missouri.   They are Christians from Illinois and their group will be made up of women, children, and inexperienced men.   We, the Omaha, will escort them, but we need your aid in giving them safe passage to the lands of the Arapaho."

Buffalo Bull rose and paced the hard, baked floor of the lodge and a cool, silent air fell over the smoky atmosphere.

"You, young son of Fontenelle, are asking me to pull warriors away from their own villages to give protection to uninvited intruders I do not know and will never see again! Explain to me, brave pride of the Omaha, what would this venture gain for my people?"

Logan recalled what his grandfather had said of the Pawnee, and without an answer he merely stood flat-footed staring at the old chief. This amused Buffalo Bull because he knew the young man had no adequate argument.

To make his point stronger, Buffalo Bull elaborated on his true feelings by saying softly: "Outline for me, charitable one, what do we as fellow natives owe the white man? You say that these people are in terrible danger from the Sioux. I sometimes feel that the Sioux harass us because we do not kill the white man. You say that we should escort these people through dangerous lands. I ask you, who has made this land dangerous? Who is the intruder who has gained the wrath of the redman for his vile deeds, lying tongue, and wasteful slaughter of the animals we depend upon for our very existence?

"Years ago this land was not considered a treacherous area full of savages. It flowed with the favors of the great Tirawa and a form of tranquility reigned. Only after the advent of the fair-skinned man did the animals disappear, one's word become worthless, and the storm sweep the calm from the prairie."

Despite all the times that Logan had thought and practiced the proper answers to the questions he had wisely anticipated, he felt totally inadequate and embarrassed now that the true test was placed in front of him. Where was his ability to think? Where was the sound logic he had learned from the Jesuits? An obvious failure who had been put down by one older and wiser, Logan could think of nothing to say. His next reaction was to pack up and leave. Iron Eye followed him as he moved quickly toward his belongings.

The earth lodge suddenly resounded with the words of the chief of seventy five years--words that would teach the two young men the most important lesson of their lives: "Who are these young dogs who run from me with their tails dragging on the ground? Is this the son of Fontenelle? Are these the cubs in line for chiefdom of the Omaha? Heaven help the future of the Omaha if they are to be led by the heart rather than by the brain."

Both Logan and Iron Eye remained silent because it was very difficult to argue with the cutting and ultimate truth. Having packed, the pair stood in front of Buffalo Bull.   "Thank you for your kind hospitality and for listening to our plea for those who are not our own," said Logan. "You have asked what we redmen owe these white settlers. I cannot agree with you more; they are the reason for many of our problems. On the other hand, we cannot just turn these helpless people over to the hazards of the prairie and we must not allow the Sioux to have a victory of this magnitude."

The words of the young Omaha quieted the old Pawnee, for undoubtedly this was the rationale he was seeking. The old veteran of many campaigns turned from Logan and Iron Eye, took a seat by the fire, and went into deep meditation. After some lapse of time, the young Omaha made their move toward the entrance, only to be halted by more words from the chief: "Your thoughts are indeed deep and wise," stated Buffalo Bull. "The great Tirawa has convinced me that you are correct and that your visit here was divinely guided." Grasping the hands of Logan, the Bull continued: "You have proven to be the son of Lucien Fontenelle and you always will be welcome here among the Grand Pawnee. Please inform your grandfather that when we receive word from you that the wagon train is heading west, we will move to meet you. We will then watch over the safety of your friends until they reach the mouth of the South Platte."

The youthful braves embraced the wise old man, took exit, mounted their ponies, and rode hastily from the village. Satisfied with themselves, Logan and Iron Eye struggled through the long ride back to Bellevue where the news of the "conquest" of Buffalo Bull was among the best ever received by the skeptical Big Elk.

When spring finally broke that year of 1847, the majority of the Mormons under the leadership of Brigham Young left Florence, Nebraska for lands to the west.   In the lengthy days that it took the small wagons to labor along the main stream of the Platte River to the junction of its south branch, accounts of the trip speak of several Indian sightings.   The very fact that the trip was made without incident was no doubt a result of the warriors of the Omaha and the Pawnee keeping a close vigil over the nearest ridge or hill.   Some of the reported sightings were no doubt of those braves in the performance of their serious task.   Had any war party been poised to strike the wagons throughout the long stretch of the river valley, their plans were thwarted by the presence of these guardians of Saints in quest of their land of plenty.

CHAPTER SIX

Paper Chief

Death came to the elderly Big Elk in the summer of 1847. The shock hit the Omaha suddenly as the chief died in his sleep, possibly from heart failure. It behooved the people to bury the chief quickly because of the warm weather and the impossibility of embalming.

Unlike most tribes of the prairie, the Omaha buried their dead, so a high site overlooking the river was chosen for the interment of the famous leader. The day of the burial was a melancholy one as many people from the area, both Indian and white, showed up to pay their respects to this wise and generous man. The chief was dressed in his robe of office and was laid on a large buffalo robe alongside his grave. For half a day, mourners passed by the body for a last glimpse of the man who had led the Omaha through much travail. The old women of the tribe wailed as the procession of people passed the body. The citizenry of Bellevue mixed with the Omaha and other Indians from the area to mourn and view the man whose fame had spread far and wide. Iowa, Pottawattamie, Oto, Osage, and Ponca, all in their best dress, looked with awe at the great man on the ground as if they felt he never could die. Only one other Omaha chief had claimed as much fame as Big Elk and that was Blackbird, who unlike his successor, was notorious for his infamy.

As the large crowd gathered about the burial site, the drums of the Omaha began beating out a tempo of lament. In a concluding act of the ceremony, four braves, stripped to the waist, began administering to the chief. These bearers of honor finished wrapping Big Elk in the colorful buffalo robe and formed the burial package by tying it with strips of raw hide. Then, using three long leather straps, they lowered their beloved leader into the earth. By custom, the job of covering the body was left to the women of the tribe.   When all the mourners had left, the wailing women filled the hole around the body with their hands.

In the early days following Big Elk's death, Great Eagle, the senior member of the Council of Chiefs, temporarily assumed the leadership of the people.   A meeting of the council was soon called to perform the task of filling the vacancy left by Big Elk.   The council met at the appointed time and found itself faced with a large dilemma.   It was the general opinion of the members that the successor to Big Elk should be one of his descendants.   If this tradition was to be followed, both Iron Eye and Logan would qualify on an equal basis because both were grandsons and the older males of their families.   The council solved the dilemma by breaking precedent, and, in an atmosphere of great joy, chose to appoint an extra member to their group. Iron Eye was picked as a "war chief" and Logan a "paper chief" because of his two years of formal education.

As a sleek, strong, intelligent, young Omaha brave, Logan looked like anything but a "mongrel" as he was tagged by the writer, Irving.   A paper chief or a scribe he was not, and of the eight chiefs of the council, he appeared to be the most hawkish.   Even though Logan lived with his family in his father's house near the trading post, the welfare and the image of the Omaha was utmost in his mind.

Now as chief, Logan was even more aware that one thousand Omaha did not command proper respect among the people of the area, particularly in the camps of the Sioux.   This above everything else irritated the young chief who, at age twenty-two, was highly respected among the Cheyenne, Arapaho, Comanche, and Pawnee.

The news of the death of Big Elk had no more than circulated through the camps west of the Missouri than the word arrived that Goes To War, the war chief of the Oglala, had succumbed to the ills of old age.   A force of fear gripped Logan as he heard the report because it required no genius to realize that Sharp Horn, arch enemy of the Omaha, would now probably command the war efforts of the Oglala. The new chief realized that time was running out for the weak Omaha people. If anything was going to be done, now was the time for action. For days, Logan contemplated the strengths and advantages of the tribe and he finally decided it was time to air his long-gathered thoughts with his fellow chiefs. Logan stood before the council after calling an emergency meeting. He was regarded as one of the best educated members of the tribe and had individually gained the respect of the majority of the Omaha tribe. So, it was not considered unusual that he should want to address the group.

"Fellow leaders," he began, "now more than ever the Omaha people need our guidance. With the death of Goes To War, the Oglala and Dakota will not be restrained in their actions against us. It is the time to act or we may be destroyed. We, the Omaha, are very weak in numbers, so we must consider our other strengths. Despite our limited numbers, we are strong in friends and relatives who have problems similar to ours. I would like to say a few things about our relatives who surround us on the north, east, and south. I do not know how our brothers, the Ponca, feel about the Sioux. At times they are at war with them and at other times they enter into treaties with them. I do know, however, that the Ponca are highly respected in the Dakota camps because of the past wars between the tribes. Whether the Ponca would support us against the Sioux is a matter of question.

"We cannot count on any support from the Iowa who occupy the area across the river. As has been shown in the past, where the Sioux are concerned, the Iowa will not lay claim to us. It appears that these relatives do not want to associate too closely with us for fear of gaining the wrath of the Santee or Dakota.

"I know from first-hand experience that our relatives to the south are truly our cousins. They are cut from the same mold as the Omaha. The Osage and the Kansa, even though they live a good distance from us, should support us in the problems we face. We have been very lax in not keeping a closer relationship with these people who are strong in numbers and long on bravery."

"As for our non-related friends, the Pottawattamie, as well as our friends and close neighbors, the Oto, would be with us in any undertaking against the Sioux. They too want to see the hunting areas open to them. Although smaller than most tribes around us, they are unsurpassed in their bravery and resistance to treachery. Even though they will not be led by us, they will support us if our cause is right.

"I do not feel that we should sit here and wait for the Oglala and Dakota to overrun us. I also do not feel that we are the only people that will suffer if Sharp Horn decides to move east in a mood of conquest. I have called this meeting with the intention of discussing the formation of a defense coalition with our relatives and friends and at this time I would like to hear some of your thoughts on this possibility." On this Logan took his seat.

Iron Eye was the first to respond to Logan's call for discussion. "How can we possibly form a federation for defense with our relatives living so far away? It seems to me that if it could have been done, our forefathers would have done it years ago."

"I believe I can speak for the older members of the tribe," spoke Great Eagle. "As long as I have been in a leadership role, the idea of a federation with our friends has never been discussed. It is, in my opinion, a good idea and should be encouraged, even though I cannot conceive a way it can be made to work."

"It is not difficult to get people to band together against a common enemy," snapped Logan as he jumped to his feet. "I have seen it work near Fort Laramie and it will work here. All I want today is permission from this council to visit with the chiefs of the Oto, Pottawattamie, Osage, Kansa, and Ponca to see if they would be willing to participate in a show of strength against the Sioux. I'll leave now so that you can discuss the idea further and take a vote."

Logan bowed and walked from the council area and into the silent woods to meditate. He scarcely had begun to concentrate on Wakonda when Iron Eye appeared next to him blurting the news that the council had approved his request to arrange a coalition of friendly tribes.

On this word, Logan was suddenly transformed from a humble worshiper before Wakonda to a haughty, proud leader of men. "This is the moment I have dreamed of for years, Iron Eye," yelped Logan. "This is our chance to bring back the dignity of our people who have suffered so long."

The young chiefs met the next day with Great Eagle in the confines of the elder's lodge. Here the format for the formation of the organization of tribes was laid out. Essentially it was agreed that the two young chiefs would visit with the leaders of the other tribes and they would try to convince them to participate in a gathering of forces.

"Explain to the chiefs, if they agree to joining in a show of strength, that there will be a massing of braves at the time of the new moon of October near the bend in the Platte River where it begins its final run to the Missouri," suggested Great Eagle. "It is important for you to understand that they will be able to release only a part of their forces in a venture such as this because they would not want to leave their villages totally unprotected."

The next months saw Logan and Iron Eye traveling the length of the Missouri from the Niobrara to the Kansas Rivers recruiting forces for the meeting in October. Their experiences were varied and their receptions ranged from cool to very warm amongst the tribes visited. The young chiefs made their final report to the older Great Eagle late in July of 1847 following their exhausting trips. Iron Eye spoke for the traveling pair: "Our report is one that probably could easily have been predicted. All the tribes that we visited responded well to our call by promising to send warriors to our rendezvous in October. All tribes, that is, except the Ponca. They told us that they had just entered into a peace pact with the Dakota and they did not care to antagonize the Sioux. We cannot blame them for not joining us because their villages are more vulnerable than any of the other tribes we approached. All in all, we feel the mission was a great success and should result in a large collection of warriors in October." Great Eagle reveled in the report.

The weeks of August proved to be extremely busy ones for the total Omaha battle force. Making plans to challenge the Sioux was no small undertaking and called for preparation of weapons, supplies, food, horses, and tipis. To gear up for battle, various offensive and defensive plans had to be devised and practiced. In this regard, the young chiefs proved to be very good tacticians. Day after day, the warriors of the Omaha met in conference with the war chiefs and spent many hours in the flood plain of the Missouri practicing battle maneuvers. This type of drill toughened the warriors and put a keen edge on their team effort.

The Omaha became the center of planning for the cooperating tribes in the immediate area. In the early weeks of September, the Omaha camp was visited by neighboring Pottawattamie and Oto and this put a new enthusiasm into the already spirited activity and attitude of the Omaha fighters. The movements of the Pottawattamie appeared very intense and calculated, exuding a subtle and fierce confidence while the Oto appeared more like the Omaha, eager to demonstrate their accuracy with the bow from speeding mounts.

Although not visited by Logan and Iron Eye, the Pawnee were the next people to respond to the call for a show of strength by making an initial call to the Omaha encampment. It has been said that early on a balmy morning in September 1847, the Omaha awakened to observe ten mounted warriors surveying their village from atop the hill to the west. It was obvious to the sentries that these were Pawnee from their dull garb and peculiar hair dressing.

When the riders knew they had been sighted, they prodded their horses down the slope and headed for the main path which wound through the large camp. As they approached the sentries, they halted on a signal from their leader, a slim, grim warrior sitting bareback on a grey and black steed. Covering his shoulders and thorax was a light-weight skin vest which when parted exposed a giant steel knife and an iron tomahawk. Tied to the neck of his horse was a long arrow pouch and stumpy bow.

"I am Mondak!" shouted the Pawnee. "I have a message for Fontenelle from the Bull." With this the sentries led the visitors to the council area at the center of the village. Here they tied their horses and rested.

Logan hurried to meet the Pawnee upon being summoned. "Welcome, Mondak, to our home village. I want you and your band to be comfortable and get plenty of rest and nourishment," offered Logan.

"Buffalo Bull sends his warm greeting to you," said Mondak. "He has learned from the Kansa that you are forming a collective force to move against the Sioux. He feels slighted that the Pawnee have not been asked to be involved. If you would want the support of the Pawnee, the chief promises that his braves will be here at the next new moon."

Logan couldn't help showing his extreme joy over these words. "Explain to Buffalo Bull that we would have invited the Pawnee to join the force, but we felt that we have already imposed too much on your people. Tell the great chief that I am elated at his decision and that our united battle group will be invincible with the Pawnee braves included at our side."

To return the courtesy that the Pawnee had shown him on two occasions, Logan invited the dark, serious-looking braves to take quarters in Big Elk's lodges and arranged to have meals prepared for them by the women of the tribe. The sun wasn't high in the sky before all the Pawnee, including Mondak, were sound asleep recouping their strength after their exhausting journey from the junction of the Loup and Platte Rivers.

The good news of the Pawnee joining the show of force spread quickly through the Omaha village. When the warriors from the west awoke from their naps, they milled about the area of the chief's lodges. Soon they became the viewing object of many curious villagers including a group of giddy young girls. Despite the attention, the proud Pawnee braves kept their usual melancholic composure and kept to themselves.

Iron Eye and Logan visited Mondak again toward evening. Gathering inside the main lodge, the young chieftains and the English-speaking Mondak exchanged compliments. Logan recalled their earlier visit to the Grand Pawnee and the lively conversation with Buffalo Bull. Mondak reviewed his participation in the combined escort efforts for the Mormons and he made sure that both Logan and Iron Eye understood the high opinion that Buffalo Bull had of them.

"We would not be here today," Mondak explained, "if it were not for the great respect our gruff old chief has for the two of you. Buffalo Bull believes that your cause is right and he also believes that the idea of demonstrating strength in a unified way will impress, as well as worry, both the Oglala and the Dakota."

"Why don't you and your men stay here for a time and see more of this beautiful river valley?" invited Logan.

"The invitation is attractive," said the rugged Pawnee leader, "but we are needed along the Platte. So, we'll leave in the morning."

As the sun rose on the next day, the Pawnee could not be seen, having left the village as the soul leaves the body.

CHAPTER SEVEN

Vengeance Moon

In the many years that the Omaha tribe fielded warrior forces, at no time had these parties been involved in the planning of an aggressive move against an enemy. All of the preparations in the past had been of a defensive nature. The fall of 1847, however, was a new time, the time of Fontenelle, time for a return to the greatness of old.

Each and every brave of the Omaha war party was impatient for the October moon, the forming of the composite battle group, and the demonstration of strength to the Sioux. Logan was no different from the rest of the young men who looked forward to the impending activities. In Logan's mind, the mission was destined for success, for to him it had been approved by Wakonda. In thinking about the coalition he had organized, Logan couldn't help imagining that perhaps this was what the Sioux had feared for years. Maybe the Sioux opposed the Omaha as they did because they felt that somewhere in this nucleus of people was the ability to organize the plains tribes against them.

Whether the Sioux believed this or not, the time had arrived for restitution. The mild activity of September turned into frenzied preparation in the Omaha camp as October approached and the moon became larger and larger. Many young Omaha even appeared to worship this celestial body as if it had some control over the action that lay ahead.

The camp near Bellevue was not the exception as the full moon approached. The camps of all tribes in the federation came alive as the time drew near to assemble on the Platte. Never before had the tribes along the wide Missouri been aroused to this degree. Elation ran so high among the Osage that their representative force left much earlier than was needed for rendezvous. Wounded Buffalo, the war chief of the Kansa contingent, in his final prayer before leading his warriors north, could hardly meditate in his anticipation of seeing the River People combined with the Grand Pawnee in challenging the Sioux.

Meanwhile in the sandhills, not far from the destination of the federated forces, camped a rather large contingent of Dakota--one of the many usually seen scattered throughout the Nebraska and Dakota Territories in the 1840's. It was situated in the upper reaches of the Elkhorn valley, about as far south and east as the Dakota ventured in their normal living routine. Only in warring efforts against the Ponca, Omaha, or Pawnee had they extended themselves beyond this point. Led by a sub-chief, Strong Hand, these people had finished a large hunt and having packed their meat, were ready to pull back to their winter quarters in the Black Hills.

On the morning that the Dakota were dismantling their quarters and loading their horses, it was reported to Strong Hand that a war party was approaching from the west. Assuming that it was made up of fellow Sioux, Strong Hand took no steps to brace for an attack. His assumptions proved to be correct as a large force of Oglala appeared on the rim of hills to the west. The party probably was composed of some two hundred and fifty rugged-looking braves sporting a wide variety of weapons.

The influence of the white man on the Oglala was evident from an occasional appearance of a rifle, a tailored coat or a dress hat. Out of the young pack suddenly appeared a muscular brave who was immediately recognized by Strong Hand as Sharp Horn. Mounting his horse, the Dakota chief rode to meet the young chieftain who had gained a fearful reputation not only among the enemies of the Sioux, but also among the various tribes within the Sioux Nation.

The two leaders greeted each other in the typical cold Sioux fashion. Sharp Horn was the first to speak. "Even though we are a strong force," he remarked proudly, "we are glad to have come upon you and your warriors. We have just learned that a large party of Pawnee has left the Loup valley in a very unusual manner. We do not know where they are headed, but if they come in this direction we plan to oppose them.   To do this we will need your help."

"The movements of the Pawnee are no concern of ours at this time," answered the older chief.   "We have just finished a hunt and have many women and children with us.   We are not in a position to think of pushing a fight with the Pawnee.   My good wishes go out to you Sharp Horn, but we must return to the hills."   The Dakota turned his horse around upon giving his refusal and sped off to return to his people.

Sharp Horn flushed with anger as he sat on his horse and watched the Dakota leader give orders to his tribesmen to move northward.   Feeling rebuked, the Oglala war chief raced back to his braves who were jeering the departing Dakota.   Enveloped in a solid vocal crescendo, the marauders sped south in a mood to attack anything that might be unfortunate to cross their path.

Once in the heart of the sandhills, it wasn't long before the Oglala band got its wish.   A day and a half after leaving the Dakota, the band sighted a small wagon train entering the area drained by Beaver Creek, a land reputed for its excellent buffalo population and claimed by the Sioux Nation.

The train of nine wagons was manned by experienced plainsmen and mountain men and an assortment of Indian scouts.   Carrying a good supply of salt, the train had a mission to secure enough buffalo meat to feed the men of an Oregon Trail cattle drive moving from the Kansas River to Fort Walla Walla.   Among the expert riflemen in the group were such famed frontiersmen as Jesse Applegate, Kit Carson, and Thomas Fitzpatrick.   Applegate, the boss of the train, was aware of the surveillance by the Oglala, but he did not close the gap between wagons or change course or speed.

"That's a good-sized group of Sioux out there," said Applegate to Fitzpatrick.   "I hope that chief doesn't think he can overrun us.   That'd be plain suicide."   Fitzpatrick nodded in agreement.

Sharp Horn and his braves rode parallel to the train for an hour studying its occupants and deciding whether or not to attack. Knowing that it would be very dangerous to bring his force into the range of the rifles of the train in the daytime, Sharp Horn decided to wait until after dark, when the train was stopped, to work his braves in closer to the wagons.

Applegate swung his wagons into a defensive circle as dusk settled in and his thirty men took up positions armed with rifles and hand guns. Although small, the train was a veritable fortress. Only an occasional brave of the Sioux party was equipped with a rifle, and Sharp Horn realized that the only chance he had of defeating the train was to overrun it or starve it out. The chief chose the latter. He ordered his men to dismount and surround the train by taking up positions in the rough, eroded areas of the terrain some one hundred yards from the wagons. Here they stayed and slept. The occupants of the train did not sleep that night because they had to anticipate an attack even though it never came.

When the sun rose the next day, the besieged hunters were tired and bleary-eyed from staring continuously into the darkness. The Sioux were rested and many of them moved about outside of rifle range. It didn't take Applegate long to determine Sharp Horn's tactics and he thought about his own alternatives. Should he stand and use up his supplies or should he make a running fight out of it? He decided to play a waiting game, at least for a time, because the wagons were well supplied with food and water. During the morning the men of the train took turns sleeping, standing watch, and anticipating the next move of the Oglala.

Sharp Horn was frustrated over the potential hazard the train presented to his men, yet eager for action he ordered his braves with rifles to fire into the circle. As a result, the remainder of the morning was spent in the exchange of rifle balls between the braves hidden in the rough depressions of sand and the plainsmen beneath the wagons.

Tom Fitzpatrick chewed on a large lump of tobacco as he sat on a powder box and peered across the Nebraska plain. He thought of how many times he had been in similar predicaments with the redmen in his long career as a guide and trapper. Turning to one of his younger companions, he attempted to lend words of encouragement and comfort.

"Looks like them redskins are just playin' a waitin' game," he chortled. "Wish they'd show themselves a little better so's we could put 'em away one by one."

The young man next to Fitzpatrick remained quiet contemplating his fate while old Tom soaked the wagon wheel with tobacco juice and continued to babble on saying: "Seems to me them injuns out there just want to starve us out. Little do they know, this bunch of prairie rats can probably last longer out here than they can. Don't look to me like they've got much in the way of supplies includin' tobacco and whiskey. Could be a long, long wait. Just wisht I could get a good bead on one of 'em to liven things up a little."

At another sector in the defensive circle, Applegate and Carson poked their loaded buffalo guns over the lowered tongue of one of the wagons. In his seated position Applegate did not show the worry contained within his huge hulk. To lend encouragement to the men in his group, he shouted instructions: "If any of them redskins puts up his head, take it off. Maybe that'll teach 'em to be more hospitable when we come a callin'." The laughter of the men broke the dead silence of the prairie and didn't help the morale of the braves lying among the cactus, yucca, and rattlesnakes.

Carson rubbed his bold mustache and peered out onto the grassland from under his slouch hat. "We need a break, Applegate. This waitin' is just too damn tough on the constitution. Something's just got to happen 'cause we sure as hell can't stay here 'til winter." Applegate agreed.

The stalemate continued through the afternoon as the Sioux and the frontiersmen became more dehydrated in the autumn sun and warm, southern wind. It was obvious from the lack of activity among the Sioux that the members of the train would spend another night in the long, long wait.

The Indian braves refreshed themselves as the sun went down with dried deer meat and with water brought up from a distant creek. On this particular night the moon was very bright and several of the Sioux began the Ghost Dance around a fire fueled with buffalo chips. A lone drummer kept up the beat as the braves continued to shuffle and chant late into the night, keeping nerves on edge within the little circle of wagons.

*   *   *   *   *

It was the strangest sight ever seen on the plains as the Osage rode with Oto and the Oto with Kansa. The Pottawattamie rode with Pawnee and the Omaha moved about the total force acquainting themselves with their newly acquired allies and encouraging them on with demands for vengeance.

> Numbers are no measure of size,
> Pottawattamie.
> You ride abreast of me and do not cower.
> You shed your blood with me and spur me on,
> Oh Pottawattamie.

None of the warriors in this party of over five hundred needed to be reminded of the strength of the Sioux. This was mostly a volunteer force and few of those in it had families who had not tasted the sting of the Dakota, Oglala, Santee, or Teton. Although here by their own choice, the braves in this composite group appeared hand-picked and they carried a variety of weapons never before seen in a single war party. Among the lances, many rifles could be seen and the horses were some of the finest on the plains. The total appearance of this war party could only be described as sleek, and potent. It was apparent that the braves in the party represented the best of their respective people.

The allied warriors crossed the Elkhorn on the third day on the trail and headed into the grassy sandhills. Most had been here before, hunting buffalo on this famed prairie that was held sacred by some. Logan and Iron Eye rode with Mondak of the Pawnee in an attempt to make him feel more at ease because there never had been very good blood between the Pawnee and the

Osage. The ill feeling between some of the tribes probably originated at a time long before any of these braves had been born, but no matter how strong the feelings, they were in each case supplanted by the basic urge to avenge the Sioux.

Most of the leaders in the united force had conversed with one another during the long ride on this very warm day. When the day's trek came to an end and the warriors began to make camp with their own tribesmen, the leaders of the various bands met on the shady slope of one of the sandhills. Here the chiefs reviewed the strategy they would use in battle under various possible circumstances in which they might engage the Sioux. In their plans the chiefs took full advantage of the areas of expertise of the different people in the war party. The horsemanship of the Kansa and the Pawnee, the bowmanship of the Osage and the Omaha and the deadly, close-in tomahawk ability of the Oto and Pottawattamie were all worked into the strategy of the collective group. From every standpoint, this force appeared awesome and the chiefs and braves portrayed that in an air of total confidence.

"Just look at that potent brigade out there," said Iron Eye to Logan as the two chiefs relaxed in the grass at sunset. "I really have a feeling of great pride for helping to organize it."

"It is a good feeling. I still can't believe that we were able to do it," spoke Logan.

So confident was the organization of warriors in its own strength that few security measures were taken to conceal its presence. Fires were common throughout the camp and prayer, singing, and dancing were prevalent everywhere.

*   *   *   *   *

The fourth day of the stalemate between the wagons and the Sioux, Sharp Horn ordered his braves to move in closer to the wagons in an attempt to increase pressure on the occupants of the circle. In carrying out this maneuver, however, two of the Oglala exposed themselves too much and were cut down by the huge buffalo guns of the hunters. News of the deaths added to Sharp Horn's frustration as he lurked outside of the fire range. At one point the chief became so infuriated that he had to be restrained by three of his lieutenants, while he cursed the Dakota for not joining him and as he damned his own tribe for not giving him more support.

Sharp Horn's feelings were somewhat eased at high noon when a small party of fifteen Dakota rode in from the north to join their brother Sioux in their siege of the tired hunters. As they first made their appearance, a tremendous roar went up from the Oglala who were highly in need of a morale builder. When the Dakota reported to Sharp Horn, they advised him that there were more Dakota in the area and that they would be joining them soon. News of possible new arrivals moved quickly among the Oglala hidden in the tall grass and this was the reason they were not alarmed later by a large war party that appeared on the top of the hill to the east.

Logan was the only chief in the first group of warriors to reach the high position overlooking the fracas below and he was quick to analyze what was going on.

"Strip off your shirts and form two lines of column," barked the Omaha chief at each band of braves as they reached his position. When all the braves were in formation, he ordered them into battle with one gesture of his arm before they or the Oglala were conscious of what was happening. The two columns of mounted warriors crashed down the slope in different directions and the composite war party quickly formed a pincers around the battle circle below. Finally aware of what had happened to them, the Oglala warriors were totally shocked as the club-wielding Pottawattamie moved into their midst crushing every skull that appeared above the grass.

Within the wagon train despair grew to utter delight when the hunters realized that the new arrivals were not just more Sioux. "By God, those savages are on our side!" bellowed Applegate.

As the battle grew among the Indian adversaries, it was easy for the riflemen of the wagon train to distinguish between their bare-chested friends and the shirted Sioux. The hunters made the most of this advantage given to them by Fontenelle, blowing huge holes in each buckskin top appearing in range. The noise of battle increased to a deafening pitch as the bowmen of the Omaha, Pawnee, and Osage moved into the grounded Sioux south of the wagons. Scream upon scream came from the ranks of these Oglala as arrows found their marks from elevated vantage points.

It didn't take long for the Sioux to panic, break, and run for their horses which had been scattered early in the fighting by the clever Mondak and a collection of Kansa warriors. In just a short while, the prairie was strewn with Oglala and Dakota bodies. Never before had the Sioux Nation suffered a defeat of this magnitude with only a handful of warriors making their escape by hiding in tall grass or in the eroded areas of the blowouts which dotted the area.

Among the very fortunate survivors was Sharp Horn, who becoming wounded in the height of the battle, crawled off into a depression in the sand that was covered well with tall grass. Here, licking his wounds like an injured wolf, he vowed to gain vengeance against the young chief who he recognized as Omaha and who led the attack that brought the Sioux to ignominy.

CHAPTER EIGHT

Encore to Exsanguination

When the last of the Oglala had been put away, extreme joy and merriment broke out among all facets of the integrated war party. Whooping and bellowing echoed back and forth across the prairie. Kansa warriors hugged Pawnee and the Osage horsemen danced their steeds in ecstatic salute to their Oto brethren. Many of the Omaha began the Victory Dance there on the plain among the bodies of the fallen enemy. Never before had the hunters of the train witnessed such a sight. The younger members of their party broke ranks to dance and make revelry with the war painted braves. It was mass approval, indeed, of a grim and deadly feat. Much of the whiskey supply of the train was turned out and passed to the celebrants, none of whom could handle it. This, of course, added more color to the dramatic and colorful event.

The leaders of the train, Applegate, Carson, and Fitzpatrick wandered through the victorious horde shaking hands and thanking the young warriors individually. Kit Carson approached Iron Eye and Logan toward dusk as the chiefs rested against their ponies that were relaxing in the soft sand and grass. Many thoughts crossed the minds of the young men as they recognized the noted plainsman. In keeping with his usual reaction to embarrassing situations, Iron Eye sat soberly and quietly showing no emotion on his stone face as Carson approached.

"Sure want to thank you men for saving our hides," said Carson to Logan as he stretched out his hand.

Instead of accepting Carson's handshake, Logan stood and saluted with raised lance in a gesture of respect, but not friendship. Surprised at this cold and unusual treatment from representatives of the Omaha tribe, Carson dropped his hand as Logan restrained himself from the urge to "run him through" for his desertion of Moneta and her children. Carson did not know, but Logan remembered how Moneta longed and wept for him following his departure.   He recalled how each evening, for years, she would ascend to the top of the high hill near the Omaha village to stare to the west and hope in vain for Carson's return.

Even though Carson did not recognize Logan and Iron Eye in their adult roles, suspicion that he had been recognized caused a feeling of guilt to pass through him.   In this state he forgot about celebrating and retired to the wagons with the thoughts and feelings that made him the most misunderstood scout in the early West.

As darkness closed in on the grassy moor, the leaders of the allied force and the train, realizing that they were in enemy country, called a halt to the merrymaking and began preparations for their own defense

In the morning the two groups decided to part company.   The leaders of the wagon train planned to get on with their original objective--obtaining buffalo meat.   Hitching up, they began their slow plodding way to the west and north.

Even though the battle brigade had completely annihilated Sharp Horn and his renegade party, they were not about to disband and go home.   They had garnered too much esprit de corps to do that.   As representatives of various ravaged tribes, they had dedicated themselves to a show of force.   Hence, the leaders decided to continue their search and destroy mission.   In so doing, the victorious force moved southwest from the battle site with plans to circle back and check on the safety of the buffalo hunters.   Several of the chiefs felt that while carrying out their mission, they could keep a protective eye on their meat-gathering friends and at the same time use them as decoys for prowling enemy.

At sunset of the first day on the move, as the warriors made camp, Logan wandered slowly to the nearest hilltop to pray.   As the sun painted a beautiful picture in the west, many deep thoughts filled his mind.   It was a long time since the Omaha chief had conversed with his maker.   Since becoming a chief devoted solely to the survival of the Omaha, he had almost forgotten his master. But here, under the reality of battle and impending battle, he felt the need to relate to Him.

"Oh Great One," Logan prayed, "you have guided me to this point in this undertaking and I have no doubt that what I have done is right in your eyes. Let me always satisfy your will and never let me forget that I am a human being with intellect and dignity. In battle set me apart from the animal and savage. In authority teach me tolerance and in triumph teach me what I have never known, compassion for the enemy."

The story carried by the Dakota to Sharp Horn that other Dakota were about to join him (before his defeat) was no false rumor. Sixty miles to the northwest of the point of departure of the train and the allied war party, another war group pushed along in typical Sioux fashion. Some two hundred strong, the band was led by the colorful Half of Moon, who, though a Dakota, possessed the same philosophy as Sharp Horn toward whites and other Indians of the eastern Nebraska Territory. Half of Moon was a forceful leader when it came to warfare and most of his followers were young, reckless braves who relished confrontation with their adversaries.

Riding fast and hard, the Dakota reached the Beaver where at nightfall they set up a camp from which they planned to operate in several direction in their search for Sharp Horn and his warriors. By stopping, they missed intercepting the wagon train that crossed the Beaver several miles to the south.

When the new day broke on the Sioux camp, the early sun rays found the Dakota braves scurrying about readying their mounts and weapons for travel and possible battle. It wasn't long before the band was joined by the middle-aged but hardened Half of Moon and they continued their surge to the southeast. At noon the Sioux drew up at the top of a sandhill from which they could overlook a large grassy area ahead of them. With the wind blowing from the south, the braves sensed an unmistakable odor evolving from the valley below. On closer inspection, it was obvious that what they were viewing was what was left of a

battlefield.   Their search for Sharp Horn and his strike force
was over.   The party gazed with amazement at the remains of a
once proud battle group.   The only movement they could see was
that of an occasional crow, hawk, or coyote claiming some midday
sustenance.

Besides being a brave chief, Half of Moon was no fool.   He
concentrated on the grim sight in the valley.   Various thoughts
began crossing his mind.   What kind of powerful force was it
that could have slaughtered the pride of the strong and
relentless Oglala tribe?   To Half of Moon there was no force in
these parts capable of inflicting such a complete victory over
his fellow Sioux.   On a signal from their chief, the Dakota rode
down the slope and through the bodies that were scattered over
the wide area.   Half of Moon thought about giving the
appropriate burial to the fallen braves, but he also realized
the task would take too long and place his men in possible
jeopardy.

As the Dakota warriors reached an eroded area to the south
of the battlefield, they were startled to see a badly injured
and bloody Sioux break out of the tall grass to meet them.   Half
of Moon recognized the brave and called out his name, but Sharp
Horn could not respond and collapsed in the sand weakened from
lance wounds and lack of nourishment.

Quickly the Dakota gathered about the fallen chief to attend
to his needs.   It wasn't long before Sharp Horn was alert and
talking profusely.   The young man related the incidents leading
up to and including the battle.   Half of Moon and his men stood
wide-eyed as he described the awesome multi-tribal task force
that wiped him out.   To the Dakota, the whole tale seemed
haunting and unbelievable.   Who in the wildest of Sioux dreams
would have imagined the gathering of the Missouri River people
with the Pawnee for offensive purposes?

"I warned your chief Strong Hand that the Pawnee were on the
move, but he would not support me," Sharp Horn told Half of
Moon.   "Yesterday morning the wagon train and the enemy parted
company," stated the wounded chief.   "The train has moved to the
west and the war party has moved to the southwest."

"It looks like our best target would be the train," answered Half of Moon, "but first we should return to camp with you."

Back at the Beaver Creek camp, Sharp Horn shared a shelter with Half of Moon. Here he attempted to discourage the Dakota chief from seeking out and attacking the buffalo-hunting train. "Even if you find the wagons, you will have the same problem we had in attacking it," said Sharp Horn. "The wagons are well-armed and the hunters are experts with the long rifle. You have no more men than I had and you will be no more successful."

Half of Moon listened to the words of Sharp Horn, but said nothing. He left the shelter to walk and consider the warning further. As he meditated on his next move, Half of Moon analyzed the total situation and he thought of the pride of the Dakota. Even though the Oglala had failed against the wagons, this did not preclude the Dakota from defeating it. The very thought of overrunning the train stimulated the warring instinct within him. Why should he listen to one who was vanquished? This was war and wars are not won by running from fear. His mind was made up and in a short while he would pursue the train.

The next day the Dakota rested, ate, and bathed in the clean waters of the creek. Half of Moon spent most of his time contemplating the best way to defeat the wagons with their strong fire power. Sharp Horn knew what was on the older chief's mind and left him alone to his thoughts. To the Dakota chief's way of thinking, a siege was out of the question. The only method that would work would be a sweeping surprise attack that would overwhelm the riflemen and keep them from firing even one volley. The chief's strategy was to locate the train, remain hidden until it was most vulnerable, such as at early morning, and then attack. This he firmly believed would bring him success.

At dawn the next morning, the Dakota pulled out of camp fully armed and leaving the convalescing Sharp Horn behind. Hurriedly they set a westerly course to intercept the train. After traveling for approximately ten miles, Half of Moon sent his scouts to the left and right as well as ahead of his battle group.

In his haste to locate the train and surprise it, Half of
Moon forgot to figure that the train also used scouts perhaps
better trained than his own. One of these was the sharp-eyed
Kit Carson who on this same day moved away from the wagons to
search for buffalo. It was customary with Carson that when he
approached a high hilltop, he would dismount and proceed to the
peak on foot. On this occasion, Carson repeated his practice
while climbing a rather tall sandhill to survey the area on the
other side. Cautiously leaving his mount behind, Carson came to
the top in a kneeling position. Here he waited and with his
keen eyes he scanned the wide area below. Before long he
sighted the lead Dakota scout who appeared as a moving spot on
the horizon. Realizing that the rider might be a scout for a
larger party, Carson waited as the rider came toward him. As
the figure grew larger, Carson's sharp eyes soon confirmed his
hunch when he vaguely identified a whole collection of riders on
the horizon directly behind the loner. Quickly Carson moved
back to his horse and rode hard to the wagon train.

The forward scout of the Dakota soon reached the hill from
which he had been seen by Carson. Reaching the summit, he
continued on in roughly the same direction as Carson. In less
than an hour the wagons were in full view of the haggard scout
peering from behind an eroded sand dune. The train was arranged
in a circle and positioned on a small rise in the middle of a
large open area giving the impression that it had been made
secure for the day. The scout turned his steed around and rode
to make his report to the Dakota chief. To the Dakota
everything was perfect--they had found the train without
alarming its occupants. They would rest and attack at sunrise.

Within the perimeter of the wagons, Carson organized the
hunters. "There's a mess of Sioux out there. If they attack
they'll probably come from the north at a time when we least
expect them, like tomorrow before breakfast. I want all of the
riflemen to arrange themselves on the northern sector of the
circle tonight and to take turns sleeping."

The plainsmen kept a vigil all night long and the leaders,
Applegate, Carson, and Fitzpatrick circulated among the younger

men giving them encouragement. Roving packs of coyotes serenaded the riflemen throughout the night as they howled at the unclouded moon.

Resting in his usual position on a powder keg, Fitzpatrick propped his rifle against a wagon tongue. Chewing on his favorite tobacco plug, he broke the silence with his characteristic chatter which tended to make the others more relaxed.

"Damned if this ain't gettin' to be a habit," he complained. "I just wish those redskins would spend more time at home with their squaws an leave us to our business. Hell, before we get back with any of this buffalo jerk, the cattle drive will be long gone for Walla Walla. I wouldn't doubt that some of those injuns are prowlin' around out there right now decidin' on how they are going to take us. I'm afraid if they decide to take us straight on, they're in for one helluva mornin'."

Time passed quickly for the Dakota and they rose while it was still very dark. Half asleep, they mounted their ponies and followed Half of Moon in the direction of the train. It was a very silent operation and even the horses seemed to know that they should not whinny. The Dakota got the first glimpse of the wagons as the first rays of sunlight began to peak across the eastern sky. When about a mile from the circle, the chief arranged his men into two lines with the braves abreast of each other. With the lines about thirty feet apart, he gave his order to ride fast and quietly at the wagons. Hoping to catch most of the hunters in their beds, Half of Moon felt confident that his braves could easily overrun the train. Swiftly and silently the two hundred Dakota rolled toward the tranquil circle with each brave clutching his most potent weapon. To the Dakota chief this was going to be a rabbit shoot and he smiled as he watched his fierce and eager braves swooping toward the white hunters.

The loud crack of the first salvo of rifle fire shattered the crisp morning air. This and the second salvo felled braves and horses on all sides of Half of Moon.   The surprise and the impact of the rifle balls seemed to stun and slow the momentum of the advancing horsemen so that their thrust toward the target was blunted causing them to veer away from the circle.   There had been no element of surprise and after Half of Moon regrouped his forces, the alternatives left open to him were few.   The Dakota had suddenly fallen into the same situation that Sharp Horn had a few days before.   To begin a running encirclement or a direct attack on the train would be suicide.   Half of Moon already had lost fifteen of his finest braves and could afford to lose no more.

The chief and his men stood out of rifle range deciding what to do while the hunters in the circle shouted insults seeking to infuriate them into another ineffective attack.   For a half hour the undaunted Dakota battled with the dilemma of choosing between their lives and their pride.

The dilemma was soon solved when to the surprise of the Dakota, the united party of warriors stood on the top of a hill overlooking the area.   Immediately, Half of Moon surmised the identity of the party and alerted his men to prepare for battle. The warnings of Sharp Horn rang in the ears of Half of Moon as he realized he had fallen into the same ambush as the Oglala.

The united chiefs peered down on the Sioux below and it was obvious to them that they markedly outnumbered their enemy. Nothing in their hearts called for sparing the Sioux who were in their predicament only because of their search for the thrill of conquest.   Had the Sioux spared the Omaha women and children on the Big Sioux River?   Had the Dakota and Oglala spared the small Pawnee villages on the Loup?   Had the Dakota given immunity to the small Oto and Osage hunting parties in this same stretch of the sandhills?   Had the Sioux raiders of the past overlooked the tiny units of Pottawattamie camped along the Missouri?

Hesitating in their eagerness to sweep at the Sioux, all of the leaders looked at Logan for the signal to attack.   With the force already in a line abreast, Logan ordered the braves to close ranks.   Then with one abrupt movement of his war ax, a terrible torrent of warriors exploded down the long, sandy slope to meet the Sioux. Even before the two forces collided, several Sioux braves fell from their mounts pierced by Omaha arrows launched from horseback at full speed. To Logan it was obvious that his men had learned well from their short association with the Comanche.

The noise of the melee was deafening as the two battle groups collided. War cries and death cries could be heard above the thunder of the horses' hoofs and the screams of the beasts that were forced to oppose each other in the raging hand-to-hand combat. Weapons, blood, clothing, and bodies were strewn everywhere in the sand. Some of the Omaha and Pawnee, who had rifles, held back from the onslaught and were merciless as they cut down the Dakota in action against their comrades.

There was no question of the outcome from the beginning. In their true tradition, the Sioux fought fiercely, but when it was obvious that they were beaten, about one hundred of the Dakota retreated to the north in chaos and without benefit of the leadership of Half of Moon who lay dead among the trampling hoofs of Pawnee war ponies. Many of the triumphant warriors were eager to pursue the defeated Sioux, but they were stalled by Logan who saw fit to keep his promise to Wakonda.

When the noise subsided and the dust settled, there was only sorrow among the victors who pulled their dead away from the bodies of the Dakota. These superior young men who had given their lives for the cause of their people were the prices paid by the united tribes for vengeance. They were the prices paid for future peace in the Missouri and Platte valleys and never again would any part of the Sioux Nation invade these sanctuaries.

Never again would the fallen young braves of the united people see their native ground as they were laid below the surface in the sands of the great Nebraska desert. The remains of the Sioux were left to the elements and the scavengers of the prairie. As for the survivors of the defeated Dakota, they paused only once in their bitter retreat to the north. In keeping with true Sioux loyalty to their own, the vanquished hesitated at the Beaver long enough to pick up Sharp Horn. Then they continued their withdrawal into the Dakota hills spreading tales of their formidable new foe led by an Omaha with some traits of a white man.

CHAPTER NINE

Meeting of the Winds

The return to Bellevue was not a joyous occasion for Logan and Iron Eye despite their victory over the Oglala and Dakota forces. They had left one of their closest friends, Big Cook, resting in the sands to the northwest. Although heralded as heroes by the Omaha-Bellevue community, the young chiefs returned home to face a different problem and a new challenge.

With the rapid expansion of whites to the west, the banks of the wide Missouri in 1848 were held as the gateway to the frontier and the lands east of that point were considered "fair game" for settlers. Regions claimed by the Iowa and Pottawattamie became heavily threatened by demands of white groups migrating to the west and the northern territory of the Omaha along the Big Sioux River was equally vulnerable. This section had not been occupied by the Omaha since the 1700's when their main village there had been nearly wiped out by the Santee Sioux.

The U.S. Government, in order to make the white settlements somewhat legal, began a program of purchasing lands from the friendly tribes to make way for the flood of settlers that was certain to come. Ever since Logan and Iron Eye were young boys they had seen United States land appraisers traversing the area around Bellevue, and so, it was not surprising to the young chiefs to have an appraiser present himself to the Council of Chiefs at their regular meeting. The appraiser, a Jonathan Pollard, had met previously with Great Eagle concerning the purchase of unoccupied lands and Great Eagle arranged to place his proposal on the agenda for consideration by the total council. Pollard presented his case: "I want to remind the council that the Omaha lands that we would like to purchase have not been used by the tribe for many, many years and it is unlikely that they will be used again. I have surveyed the package and I estimate that it amounts to about twenty five square miles. I do believe that the government would be willing to pay the Omaha about three thousand dollars for their rights to this land parcel."

A hush fell over the chiefs as they contemplated the matter. Great Eagle was the first to speak: "I feel that this council should give serious thought to the sale of the land in question. We have not used this territory since the last century and I do not feel that we will ever return to it. The offer by the U.S. Government will not make us rich, but it will give the people a source of money for future needs."

"I do not think that the offer as it exists now is sufficient," said Iron Eye. "Pollard's offer is less than twenty cents an acre and that would amount to only three dollars for each member of the tribe. I would be in favor of the sale, but we must have more money."

"I have something to add," said Logan, the paper chief. "While we are considering this issue with a government representative, I feel that in our bargaining we also should consider the white farmers who have settled on Omaha lands here at Bellevue. It is my opinion that in our negotiations we should work to be paid for these impositions or for resettlement of these people to lands owned by the government. Furthermore, I never have seen the lands of which we speak. I would like to visit them and then give you my opinion."

The rest of the council appeared to agree with Logan and Iron Eye that more thought and negotiation should be undertaken before a sale of the land was agreed upon.

To this Pollard responded: "I want to thank the council for taking the time to consider the government's offer. I will be back in a month to see what you have decided. If an agreement can be reached, I will invite some important officials to the final signing to show its importance to the United States."

Logan began arranging for the trip to view the northern Omaha lands the day following the meeting with the other chiefs. The older members of the tribe had lived on the land in question, but neither Logan nor Iron Eye knew anything about it. Logan decided to make the trip alone because Iron Eye was still treating his wounds of battle.

The paper chief was making his way north along the Missouri as the sun rose the next day. His plan was to cross the river using the services of a ferry the Mormons had constructed at Florence. It has been told by several frontiersmen, who were on the ferry that day, that Logan approached the boat waving and riding at full speed. The story has it that before Logan reached the river bank, the ferry pulled away. To the surprise of the passengers, and to show his disdain for the ferry operators, the bronze chief rode his steed into the river. Urging his horse to swim into the current, Logan eventually passed the ferry and beat it to the opposite bank. By the time the ferry landed, Logan and his horse were off on the second leg of the trip upriver.

"Who and what was that?" shouted one of the frontiersmen.

"Believe that was young Fontenelle, son of the Bellevue trapper," said another. "He sorta represents a new spirit among the young braves in the area. I'm afraid we ain't seen the last of him and his kind for a long while."

The young leader set a northerly course after shaking off the river water and he stayed on the flats at the water's edge where the travel was easy and game plentiful. On and on he trudged into the chilly north winds of early November. Moving by day and resting by night in any shelter he could find, Logan made good time up the broad and flood-scarred river valley.

After four sleeps, Logan passed the bluffs close to the river's edge and then suddenly the river turned in a westerly direction. Soon Logan detected the entry of a smaller stream into the river. This was it--the Big Sioux River. Arriving at its mouth, the young chief turned his mount north and moved into the area claimed by his tribe. The grass was still thick and green for this late in the year. The water in the lakes and river was deep blue and loaded with ducks and geese headed south on their annual migration. Surveying the area made Logan feel comfortable and rich. To think that the Omaha had once left this lush area seemed unbelievable. Indeed a powerful and sinister threat must have forced that exodus.

It was easy for Logan to see why the federal government would want this oasis for the white settlers. What baffled the young chief was why settlers, either white or red, had not occupied the area earlier. Perhaps the infamous deed that had occurred here left a haunting air which discouraged settlement by others. At any rate, it was Logan's assessment that the offer made by Pollard seemed far short of the true worth of the valley.

Logan spent the rest of the day riding and investigating parts of what he estimated to be the Omaha claim. Conveniently, toward the end of his rounds, Logan found an abandoned earth lodge which would serve him well come sunset. After leading his horse into the lodge, Logan set about gathering wood for the fire pit. Following some deep thought while staring into the flames and after eating some buffalo jerk, Logan fell fast asleep in his warm deerskin roll.

Awakened abruptly by two quick kicks to the shoulder, Logan opened his eyes to see that he was surrounded by five warriors he could not identify. The fire had long since gone out and from the light passing through the open lodge door, it was obvious that it was morning. Standing up, Logan studied his captors who had already confiscated his weapons. Who were these strangers? They obviously were not Santee or Yankton. They resembled Pawnee yet were not Pawnee.

Logan was ordered through gestures to leave the lodge and mount his horse. Once mounted themselves, the strangers motioned to Logan to follow. Down the Big Sioux they rode until reaching the Missouri. They then crossed the Big Sioux and proceeded west along the north bank of the Missouri. The travelers reached their destination by nightfall--an earth lodge village which apparently was home base for the captors. As he studied the village and its occupants, it finally dawned on

Logan that these "northern Pawnee" were the Arikara ("Rees"), although he would have expected to find them farther upriver.

Logan was led to an empty lodge and locked in. With scarcely any light, he groped about until he stumbled over a log on the floor. Soon he was able to muster more wood and before too long, using his flint and steel, he had a small fire going for light as well as warmth.

Contemplating his fate before the flames, Logan had his meditation rudely interrupted by a group of loud Arikara braves at the door. Logan recognized the eldest of the group as the leader when they entered the serenity of the earth lodge. In almost perfect Siouan tongue, which Logan understood, the spokesman began the conversation: "I am Hotok, one of six chiefs of the Arikara. You must be either Iowa or Ponca."

"I am White Horse of the Omaha," answered Logan who was somewhat relieved at having someone to converse with.

"Omaha?" the chief queried. "What is a descendant of Blackbird doing along this stretch of the Missouri? Omaha do not hunt this area nor do they have any dealings here."

"The Omaha do have an interest in this territory," Logan countered. "The valley where I was captured is our old home and still is claimed by the Omaha."

Hotok seemed surprised as he digested Logan's words. "The land along the Big Sioux has not been occupied for many years," he mused. "Our people have been thinking of settling on it for a long time to avoid the reaches of the Dakota."

"It would do you no good to build your lodges on that land," snorted Logan. "Already the white man's government has made us an offer of purchase for the white settlers who soon will occupy it."

A red flush came over the face and hands of Hotok and he shook in obvious rage. "We, the Arikara, are in desperate need of lands on which to locate," he blurted, "and you are selling to white men? I should split your skull with this war ax."

"I am sorry that the sale will spoil your plans, but the lands are not yours to take," Logan explained. "It seems to me that if you need lands and more protection, you should join your Pawnee cousins on the Platte. I know they would welcome you with open arms."

"I need the advice of an Omaha like I need more Dakota," growled Hotok as he stormed out of the lodge.

*   *   *   *   *

It was early morning and most of the Rees were asleep as "Big Jim" Bridger and his party rode past the array of tipis, bark huts, and earth lodges that comprised the village. Those Arikara who watched did not appear alarmed at the presence of the frontiersmen because the Rees, like the Pawnee, generally had a good relationship with whites. Hotok and several Arikara braves rode forward to greet Bridger as he and his party pulled into an open area just next to the village.

"Greetings, Bridger, I welcome you in the name of the Arikara and hope that this will be a lengthy visit," stated Hotok.

"It is good to be here, chief," replied Bridger. "We have had a long trip down the Missouri and would like to rest several days before moving on to Bellevue. I didn't expect to see the Arikara here any longer because the Mandan told us you were moving."

"I am afraid we will not be moving to the lands we had in mind," Hotok reported. "Several things have happened to change those plans. I suppose for total peace of mind we should join my cousin Errand Man and the Skidi Pawnee on the Platte." With these words the grim-looking chief mounted his horse saying, "Get some rest, Bridger. I will be back at sundown and we will talk some more." Hotok then turned his steed around and rode slowly back into the maze of structures that made up the village.

It was a typical November day along the north Missouri with the sun shining brightly and a touch of green remaining on many of the trees. Things were very quiet in the Ree village and only a few crows could be heard in the groves along the river. Occasionally, robed persons could be seen moving about the village.   Buffalo hides in their stretchers stood in front of many of the huts and tipis.   Through the day various hunting parties returned to the encampment with deer or antelope tied across pack horses.   The Rees lived warmly and ate well, but obviously were concerned about their future.   This was the main issue on Hotok's mind when he returned to Bridger's camp after dark for consultation with the famous pathfinder.

"I do not understand the Sioux," Bridger told the chief. "In all of our contacts with them north and west of here they appear to be content and have good relationships with their neighbors the Crow, Shoshoni, and Blackfeet.   It is only in this area that they seem to be restless.   The only thing the Dakota and Oglala seem to have on their minds is the challenge they are receiving from the tribes south and east of here.   It is reported that the Omaha, Pawnee, Osage, and others are riled up and I guess a force made up of these tribes punished the Sioux pretty well recently.   I think that your idea to move south to join the Pawnee would be a wise one.   The Sioux are nursing their wounds right now and I doubt that they will be making more raids toward the Platte and the Loup."

"Perhaps I have misjudged the Omaha," said Hotok.   "Maybe they are not the enemy we have always pictured them to be."

"I don't understand," muttered Bridger.   "The Rees have nothing to fear from the Omaha any more."

"I now hold an Omaha prisoner in the village," said Hotok. "He has told us that his people are selling the land on the Big Sioux, which the Omaha still claim.   We had planned on settling there and this is the main reason why we must think of joining the Pawnee."

All was quiet as Big Jim assimilated what he had just heard.   "I can't understand why you would want to hold an Omaha," he grunted.   "I hope you will let me see him in the morning so that I can work out your differences."

Having no good argument against Bridger's suggestion, Hotok consented to a morning meeting with the prisoner.   "I agree to this, Bridger, because the news that you bring about the Sioux defeat is good.   It gives me a different feeling about the prisoner.   Perhaps the Oglala and Dakota are now so concerned about the Omaha that they will let us move in peace."

It was early morning when Bridger presented himself at the lodge of the Arikara chief.   Shortly thereafter, the mountain man and the chief approached the lodge housing young Fontenelle.   The two guards at the entrance gave way to the pair and they entered the crude structure.   Logan was merely keeping warm by a small fire and he did not acknowledge the two figures as they approached him.

"White Horse," called Hotok.   "There is someone here to see you."   Surprised, Logan turned to view a face he had never seen before.   The tanned face, the long hair, and the clothing of the frontier all tended to stretch Logan's imagination about the identity of the stranger.

"I understand that you are Omaha," said Jim.   "How are my good friends Big Elk and Lucien the fur trader?"

"They are both dead," blurted Logan.   "Who are you to ask about their welfare?"

"Well who are you?" bellowed Jim who was amazed at how well the Indian spoke and carried himself.

"I am White Horse, a sub-chief under Great Eagle," Logan railed.   "I am on a mission for my tribe and they will not appreciate this insult to me."

Bridger chuckled inside at Logan's words.   He fully understood the peace-loving nature of the Omaha and that these harsh words were the mutterings of youth.

"Now don't ruffle your feathers, young man," said Bridger assuringly.   "I am here to help you if I can.   My name is Jim Bridger and my men and I have just finished an exploring trip up the Powder River for the government and we are on our way home to Missouri.   I am sorry that Lucien Fontenelle is dead because we were great friends.   He and I spent a lot of time together in the early fur-trading days and I was planning to see him when we reached Bellevue."

"You need not tell me about Lucien Fontenelle, Bridger. He was my father and I miss him more than I can say," uttered Logan.

Bridger's mouth dropped in total amazement at Logan's words. "I might have guessed," said Jim. "Only Fontenelle's son would have your polish out here in the wilds."

"I think you should give White Horse his freedom," requested Bridger as he turned to Hotok.

Hotok only nodded and stepped to one side as Logan and Bridger made their way to the entrance. Logan remained cold toward the Ree chief once he was outside. Grasping the reins of his horse, he waited for Bridger and Hotok to finish their conversation and then the two new friends walked lazily to the explorer's camp.

"I can't believe it, running into Lucien's son out here--it seems almost impossible that it could happen. I knew by this time that Big Elk probably was dead, but I am surprised that Lucien is gone so soon," explained the big man. "It's a terrible loss."

Logan didn't comment on Jim's words. He only hung his head and tried to think of more pleasant things. When they entered camp, Bridger took great pride in introducing Logan to everyone. Logan needed and basked in the friendly environment of the rugged, jovial frontiersmen after his bad experience with the Arikara.

Logan shared a shelter with Jim for three nights and then joined the party when it left the Arikara and moved east and south along the Missouri. The Omaha chieftain rode by himself as the party reached the Big Sioux River. This allowed him to do some deep thinking concerning this fertile valley and the incident which drove his people from it.

Logan boiled with anger as he thought of the near annihilation his people suffered here at the hands of the Santee. It was hard for Logan to stomach the fact that the Santee still lived comfortably to the north and that they had never suffered for their nefarious deed.

The majority of the party was jubilant as they moved south thinking about civilization once again. The young Omaha chief, however, remained glum with only thoughts of revenge to occupy his mind. He did not consider himself as an avenger, but as he dwelt on the subject, it was clear to him that the Santee were true enemies of the Omaha--even more so that the Oglala and Dakota.

One night in the long march down the Missouri, Logan confided in the old veteran, Bridger, about the subject of the Santee. Jim had known of the Omaha defeat on the Big Sioux, but he was puzzled that such deep and serious problems should bother a man as young as Logan. "Thoughts such as these should not be your concern, Logan," he cautioned. "A young man such as yourself should only be concerned with things such as hunting, fishing, and marriage. Dwelling on revenge will totally occupy your thoughts and ruin you in the end. The Santee affair happened many, many years ago and those responsible are gone now or are very old. You should forget it."

"I can't forget it," explained Logan. "My people were scarred for years from the incident and it took many years for them to recover. We should grind them into the sand as we did the Oglala and the Dakota."

Jim was amazed as he concentrated on what he had just heard. Becoming curious, be began to quiz the chieftain for more facts: "Recently, as we passed through the camps of the Oglala and the Dakota to the west of here, we heard many tales about the recent skirmishes between the Sioux and some allied tribes led by a half-breed. Are you telling me that you were involved in those fights out there in the grasslands?"

Logan knew that Jim would discover the truth soon enough, so he nodded humbly.

"I don't believe it," roared Big Jim. "Next you'll tell me that you are the half-breed chief who cut up the Sioux so badly."

Logan nodded saying, "In reality, it was just a matter of surprising the enemy on two occasions. It probably was a terrible shock to those who never before had tasted defeat."

"Well, I'll be a skinned donkey!" roared Bridger. "This is unbelievable! The Sioux say that you struck like an evil wind, without warning and that you now have half of the plains Indians aroused against them. Hell, it's no wonder you want to take on the Santee."

Logan took time in the evenings to relate in detail the stories of the two battles to the Bridger party, and in so doing, held the rugged frontiersmen in complete astonishment. The story sessions appeared to make the trip a little shorter and four days after leaving the Arikara, the expedition arrived at the Fontenelle property near Bellevue.

After a three day rest and after stocking up on provisions at the trading post, the Bridger pathfinders left the company of the Fontenelles to finish the last leg of their journey to Missouri. As with so many other notables who had influenced his life, Logan bade Jim Bridger goodbye, never again to have the enjoyment of his presence.

Logan picked up his duties as paper chief upon his return and also made the report of his trip to the Council of Chiefs at their regular meeting. Here he recommended sale of the land with the provision that the price be doubled and that the transaction be delayed until the end of the following summer.

The council did not understand the reason for the delay, but accepted it and voted unanimously to go along with the recommendations.

Chief Fontenelle took full advantage of the time gained through the decision of the council during the long, cold days of the winter of 1848. In this time he designed his strategy to use the distant lands of the Big Sioux to attain satisfaction against the Santee.

CHAPTER TEN

Freedom for the Bold

The stories of most wars have been told and retold, but the struggle of the Omaha people has never been placed in print before this writing. By the first weeks of 1849 most of the leaders of the Omaha, including Iron Eye, were occupying their time with the administrative affairs of the tribe. Ironically, the paper chief, the best educated, was the only one concerned with the security of the people and vengeance for atrocities committed against the tribe. This was natural because he was born into the clan of the tribe known for its displeasure toward injurious acts inflicted by other people.

Although Logan was only twenty-four years old at this point, many of the elders of the tribe looked with pride upon this young man with lighter skin. To them, Logan was held as something of a messiah who had liberated the Omaha from the threat of Sioux ambition. The people of the Omaha now moved freely, appeared prouder, and were more confident in their dealings with the whites and other tribes. They were the Omaha of old. They had found their self respect again.

The Omaha in 1849 numbered only one thousand souls with less than five hundred warriors. Despite this, and the fact that he had been reared in a normal family environment, Fontenelle's appetite for retaliation remained unsatisfied and he continued to write his purple chapter of war against the enemies of his people. Already he had struck fear into the hearts of the northern marauders and in his mind there was no reason to cease. Under the Jesuits he had learned of temporal punishment and he would be the one to deliver this penance to the Santee Sioux.

In the long hours of winter meditation, Logan convinced himself that whatever problems the Omaha had with the Santee, they were not the concern of their allies. He could not ask the

Pawnee, the Oto, or the Potawattamie to fight the private battles of his tribe. The young chief estimated that in spite of the heavy toll taken by small pox in the Santee camps, they probably still had more than one thousand braves in their force. With less than half that many Omaha warriors, he realized that any action against the Santee would have to be in the nature of a surprise and punitive in a less than absolute manner.

Logan was fully aware of the dangers of approaching Santee country with a large detachment of fighters, but he also was aware of some of the advantages that the Omaha might have in a planned operation against this branch of the Sioux Nation.

When spring broke for good, Logan initiated a strenuous program to put the warriors of the tribe into fighting shape. Within one week it was apparent that the braves of the Omaha had not lost any of their riding ability or their deadly accuracy with the bow. Day after day the young chiefs put the warriors through their paces on the flats near Bellevue. From the activity, it was apparent to the rest of the tribe and the citizens of Bellevue that big plans were in the making, but they were kept locked in the mind of the deep-spirited Fontenelle.

Logan meditated and prayed for weeks for a vision on how to proceed against the Santee, but also for weeks, nothing was made known to him. Perhaps, he thought, Wakonda did not look too favorable upon the vengeance in his heart and the whole plan of retaliation. When would the message come and in what form?

The cool days of spring soon passed into the hot and humid days of summer and still Fontenelle could not state a definite plan to his men. The warrior force had been honed to a fine edge, but with no activity or challenge they soon began showing signs of becoming rusty and dull. A fighting group or any team reaching a peak in practice drills must be used soon or it will crumble from problems of morale and dissension, and in this regard, the battle-hardened, young force of the Omaha was no exception.

The answer to Logan's problems of indecision arrived one day as the weathered mountain man, Louisiana, emerged from the oak

forest which surrounded the Fontenelle homestead. The rugged
veteran of many tours to the great north country looked quite
lonely without his usual partner Pierre DeSmet, the Blackrobe,
who already had left the frontier for semi-retirement at
Florissant.

Logan was delighted to see his old friend and welcomed him
into his home where Bright Sun prepared her usual excellent
dishes for visitors of importance. Louisiana ate heartily, and
as before, was very vocal about his latest trek into the
northern wilderness. "Why, in that north country you can canoe
for several hundred miles from one lake to another. The fish
there are as big as Louisiana alligators and you can saddle and
ride the mosquitoes," said the big man.

On and on the mountain man chattered about the clear
northern waters, the fishing, and the Chippewa people. But
then, as he wound down his tale in discussing his return trip,
the story became more interesting to Logan as he told of passing
through the camps of the Yankton, Santee, and Ponca and his
conversations with the leaders of those tribes.

"Tell me what you learned in your visit to the Santee,"
urged Logan.

"Well, my reception was a bit cool," answered Louisiana,
"but, I did have a lengthy conversation with Tall Knife who is
rather hostile. He blames the white man for the plagues that
have reduced his numbers considerably, possibly to about two
thousand people."

Fontenelle continued to query the hulk of a man that totally
filled Lucien's favorite old chair. "What does Tall Knife think
about the threat of migration of the whites into his lands?"
asked Logan.

"Don't believe he's bothered too much by that at the
moment. But he did tell me that he heard that the whites were
interested in the fertile acres along the Big Sioux which his
people won in battle many years ago. He is quite disturbed
about this and plans to send a contingent of warriors to protect
the place from occupation."

Logan was outraged as he thought about Tall Knife's words. "Won in battle against women, babies, and old men," he shouted. "We'll see what they can win in a fight with experienced warriors!"

"You mean you would consider tangling with the Santee?" questioned Louisiana in amazement.

"The Omaha have been in conflict with the Sioux before and have come out the winner," answered Logan. "With the right preparation and equipment, I believe we could defeat a large force of Santee. Some time ago a trapper named Talmadge passed through Bellevue and he carried a new weapon called the 'double-barreled shotgun' which he purchased in Saint Louis. It is loaded at the breach and at close range it is deadly. Why, if I could obtain six or seven of those weapons, I would meet the whole Sioux Nation."

"I am sure that you couldn't buy one of those if you went to Saint Louie, son," the visitor commented. "They wouldn't think of sellin' one of those to a redskin."

"Yes, but you are going there and you could buy several of them if I gave you the cash," suggested Logan.

"I don't know how ethical that would be. You know the government is trying to keep all guns out of the hands of the injuns," said Louisiana.

"Don't talk to me of ethics, Louisiana. I know that DeSmet lived by Jesuit ethics and maybe some of that rubbed off on you. But, how ethical were the Santee when they slaughtered our people along the Big Sioux?"

"All right, don't get your skin in an uproar," Louisiana agreed. "I'll buy those irons and loads for you if you'll include just a little extra money for a good night of celebration in the big town."

Before Louisiana could change his mind, Logan hurried to another section of the house and returned with a small leather sack of coins, which probably represented his share of the sale of Lucien's business.

"Here, this should take care of the guns and shot and also let you live well for a few days," Logan pressed. "Promise me,

Louisiana, that you will buy the guns before you do any celebrating in the town. Also, that you will not tell DeSmet about my plans. If the Blackrobe found out what I plan to do, he'd come upriver with his heart bleeding for the Sioux."

"I'll catch the next keelboat downriver and be back in five weeks with those irons," said the gruff, old explorer as he tucked the gold beneath his shirt.

As the frontiersman left the Fontenelle home for the settlement of Bellevue, Logan was in ecstasy about the opportunity to face an equal contingent of Santee and his own idea to add shotguns to the armament of the Omaha. In his heart, Logan wished that he already had his equipment and could leave immediately for the north country.

In a few days, Logan watched his great friend board the keelboat named the "Kansas Witch" at the Bellevue landing and then stared after the river craft until it disappeared down the fast-flowing Missouri. The weeks that followed were real torture for the paper chief. He could think of nothing but Louisiana in the big city with his money. Would he be able to buy the guns that would give the Omaha an edge over the Santee? Would he be robbed of the gold and not be able to make the purchase?

Recognizing that Logan was preoccupied with a weighty problem, faithful Iron Eye took over working with the warriors trying to keep them in top physical and mental condition. This was a very difficult task and really required a more outgoing image like Logan and not the reserved, introverted personality represented by Iron Eye. Iron Eye, however, worked hard at his self-appointed job and did well in keeping the force together and the morale high. As a result, the warriors looked as ready for action as any in the fighting history of the Omaha.

Without warning on a warm July morning, the river boat "Yellowstone" put in at the Bellevue landing finishing the first leg of its trip up the Missouri from Saint Louis. Louisiana was not on board, and when Logan learned this, a feeling of panic fell over him. So intense was the paper chief that at one point he considered taking the next boat to Saint Louis to find the big man.

With the lack of people such as Lucien, Big Elk, Big Snake, and Prince Max to confide in, Logan matured during the days that followed, learning that patience is one of the virtues for good leadership.

Another lesson which Logan learned during his long wait was that you never can predict the actions of an independent character such as Louisiana nor can you predict how he might perform a task. Expecting that Louisiana would arrive from downriver by river boat, Logan was completely aghast as he watched Louisiana enter the Omaha camp one warm afternoon leading an ox-driven wagon owned by a migrant family from Illinois.

"Just didn't trust them river rats with my valuable cargo, chief. So here it is, a little late, but totally intact," explained the Frenchman as he pointed to two large wooden boxes at the rear of the wagon.

Logan was elated. He hugged the huge frame of the adventurer then quickly recruited several burly braves to unload the boxes and store them in the lodge of Big Elk, now Logan's home within the camp. With two guards posted at the door of the lodge, Logan invited Louisiana to his Bellevue home for a good meal and some celebration.

"I brought enough ammunition along with those weapons to wipe out the Russian army," explained Louisiana as he toasted Logan with a cup of wine. "When I wake up in the morning, I'll teach you and some of your boys how to operate those scatter guns." That night Louisiana slept in the best of the Fontenelle beds and enjoyed again the best of Bright Sun's meals.

The valley to the south of the Omaha village roared from the reverberations of Logan's newly acquired "pieces" as Louisiana lectured and demonstrated their use. Time after time, the rugged pathfinder blew huge holes into a deer skin target as he showed the proper loading and handling procedures for the awesome weapons to a hand-picked group of braves. Needless to say, all of the warriors including Logan were highly impressed and very eager to fire the weapons on their own. Fontenelle passed out the guns to those he felt could best use and protect them. Then, following Louisiana's instructions, the rest of the day was spent practicing on targets both moving and stationary. The addition of the guns to the armament of the Omaha added even more to the confidence and pride of the battle group and, of course, to Logan's confidence in his ability to carry punishment to his enemies.

The following week, Logan, Iron Eye, and the warriors prepared feverishly for their expedition to the north. On the day before they were to move out, Louisiana visited Logan at the lodge of Big Elk and bade him goodbye. "I won't be going with you on your visit up north, Logan. Figure I better see what's goin' on out in the mountains," said the large explorer. "Besides, I feel it's better for me if I stay out of the injun feuds." After receiving an intimate embrace from Logan, the big man fastened his rifle and pack on his well-rested horse and, after mounting, followed the path to the west taken by so many other Bellevue visitors who were part of Logan's experience.

*   *   *   *   *

Once again the search and destroy pack, some four hundred warriors of the Omaha, was on the prowl. It had been a long time since they had engaged in battle, but bristling like a legion of Troy, they crossed the wide Missouri and moved brazenly to the north unimpressed by the knowledge of Santee numbers or reputation. Only a Logan Fontenelle could have led this light brigade into the Big Sioux valley of death and only Fontenelle could have convinced them that they would emerge victorious.

Once the force had moved fifty miles up river, they proceeded only by night and rested by day in the bluffs at riverside. Within twenty miles of the Big Sioux River, Logan and Iron Eye left the warrior group to scout for the whereabouts of the Santee. Moving quietly and carefully, Logan and Iron Eye approached the Big Sioux by night. From a high promontory, they surveyed the river as it sparkled in the moonlight.

"Can't see any camp fires so no one seems to be occupying the valley," said Iron Eye as the pair scanned the area below.

The chieftains slept at their high position until daybreak when they set out to finish their reconnaissance in the valley. Neither Logan nor Iron Eye was very fearful as they carried out their search because each was equipped with one of the new guns purchased by Louisiana. Convinced that they were the only human beings in the valley, the chiefs began studying the terrain to find the proper spot to fit their battle plan. Strangely enough, the elevated site which they first used to survey the valley, and the flat, clear area directly below it, figured strongly in their plans. After a good night's sleep, the pair returned to the rest of the braves who had remained quietly hidden away in a thickly vegetated hollow in the Missouri bluffs.

Logan surveyed his camp of fearless, muscular warriors on the day following his return and then ascended to the nearest hilltop to pray. "Oh, great Wakonda, please listen to this humble person. I know that you approve of this undertaking because of the course of events that have led up to it. Please be with us, guide us, and give us strength and bravery to carry out our plan."

When night fell on the valley of the Missouri, the well-armed braves of the Omaha left their bivouac and proceeded upriver by moonlight. Going was difficult at night on the rough terrain, but before the first rays of sunlight appeared in the East, the brigade had made good progress and again sought seclusion in the hills that skirted the Missouri River.

As night fell again, the Omaha force continued its move. They reached the Big Sioux while it was still dark and guided by their chiefs, they found cover before the sun rose again. Early in the morning, Logan dispatched three braves to scout to the north for signs of other humans. When they returned with nothing to report, the chiefs moved their men to the flats immediately below the prominent site they had found in their first visit. Here on this level strip of ground, which could only be approached conveniently from the north, Logan was to set his trap.

"I want four different pits dug evenly spaced across the width of this flat," barked Logan at the braves, "and I want a tipi built at the edge of each pit."

When the first job was completed, more tipis and bark huts were constructed to the south of the pits simulating a small Omaha village.

Once all of the work was finished, four braves assigned shotguns were ordered to live in the tipis at the edge of the pits. Four other warriors were assigned to these tipis to help stand watch, maintain fires in the camp and generally assist the gunmen. The rest of the striking force and their mounts were ordered to take positions at the top of the high ground just east of the camp. A rather large depression on the summit furnished an ideal site where the warriors could bivouac and stay out of view.

In the days that followed, various braves took their turns as lookouts from atop the hill scanning the valley for oncoming Sioux. The high position was a tremendous vantage point for the Omaha and it appeared that nothing could move along the river without being detected.

"Things have gone well for us so far," said Logan to Iron Eye on a day they served as lookouts. "We are lucky that Tall Knife didn't send a contingent to occupy the valley before we arrived."

Logan had hours to ponder about the decoys and the trap he had set for the Santee during the long wait on the hill. He knew that the Sioux were bound to infiltrate into the valley soon. In his wait, Logan often prayed and meditated on honor, pride, and death. To the Omaha, death was not too much to pay for the honor and pride of the tribe. To them, death was the great equalizer--the common denominator of life. Believing this, Logan was not hesitant about leading his braves into battle against a foe who had humiliated his people in the past.

On the thirteenth day of the wait, in early afternoon, a lookout excitedly approached Logan shouting, "We have just sighted the movement of horses and men about three miles to the north."

"Hurry to the bottom of the slope and alert the men there to stoke their fires and to man the pits with their guns," Logan told the lookout.

As commander of the battle group, Logan hurried to the Omaha braves assembled in the depression.   "Arm yourselves with warclubs and the long bows and stand by your ponies!" he ordered.

Moving to the positions occupied by the lookouts, Logan and Iron Eye scanned the valley. A long column of riders could be seen slowly closing on their position.

The force of some two hundred braves led by the Santee sub-chief, Four Wings, moved cautiously over the rough terrain riding in and around the trees along the river. All members of the Santee party seemed very alert, having traveled only a few miles from their last camp.

In true Sioux fashion, all of the braves appeared battle-experienced and moved with great confidence. The ages of the party ranged from very young to hardened veterans of many campaigns. The weapons carried by the Sioux were widely varied with knives, lances, tomahawks, bows, and an occasional rifle making up their armament.

The movement of the column came to a sudden halt as their forward scout reported the sighting of smoke to Four Wings. When more scouts were sent out, the report came back of the presence of the small village on the flats ahead. Four Wings worked his men slowly up to the edge of the flat about three hundred yards from the simulated village.

Seeing this activity, Logan and Iron Eye alerted their forces hidden on the hilltop.

Viewing a quiet village, Four Wings could think of nothing but surprise and he ordered his braves to attack swiftly. Horses lunged forward along the flat ground carrying Santee braves with conquest their only objective. The Omaha could have asked for nothing better. From among the war whoops and the rumble of stampeding hoofs, eight loud concussions could be heard in rapid succession and several of the on-rushing Santee and their steeds hit the earth as if meeting an invisible wall. Panic struck the middle and rear groups of advancing Sioux as the Omaha gunmen in the pits reloaded.   Before the surprised Santee realized what had happened to them, seven more bronzed soldiers were put down bleeding next to their mutilated horses in the grass.

Logan readied his eager brigade at the edge of the slope above the stunned, bloodied cavalry below.   Raising his shotgun high above his head, Logan gave his command: "These are Santee. Let's give them to the devil!"

On one gesture with his gun, the "mongrel" sent his pack straight for the jugular vein as four hundred Omaha braves rumbled down the slope toward the Santee.   Shocked, but not wavering, the Santee in true Sioux fashion braced for the fight.   With high momentum, the Omaha warriors smashed into the motionless enemy.   Screams and the clash of weapons filled the valley.   Horses whinnied loudly as their riders slashed away at each other.   For over ten minutes the Santee held their ground, with the more hardened soldiers setting an example for the younger men.   Soon the superior numbers and guns of the Omaha began to make the difference and the Sioux pulled back to the north, the only open escape route from the ambush.   Felled horses and braves dotted the whole width of the flat ground as a result of the separate duels that had been set up in the course of the battle.   When it was obvious that the Santee were giving ground, Logan continued to exert pressure because he knew his enemy had attacked the little "village" in the same manner it had attacked another village years before.

In order to keep from being completely wiped out, the Santee chief held his party together as a fighting unit and soon began an orderly retreat, leaving over half of the original force dead or dying on the flats.   Seeing this development, the young Omaha chiefs recalled their attacking warriors, allowing the Santee to fall back to the north country to lick their wounds and mourn their many dead. The trap had worked in an ingenious way. The punishing arm of the Santee, impatiently eager for conflict, had been severed at the elbow and what remained withered back into the Dakota Hills with no further appetite for battle.

Fifteen Omaha lay among the bodies of the Santee. Certainly more would have fallen if the element of surprise had not worked so effectively. Despite the hurt over loss of their comrades, many of the Omaha were in a jubilant mood. It was over! The people had avenged the defeat of old by crushing the cream of the Santee forces and thwarting forever the ambitions of this tribe in the area.

The Omaha prepared appropriate burials for their fallen comrades during the rest of the day. The next day, the descendants of the earlier Big Sioux humiliation filed down the Missouri valley breathing the air of freedom, which ironically since the beginning of the human race, has had to be purchased dearly with life, blood, and lingering tears.

CHAPTER ELEVEN

Bad Medicine

With the reputation of the vigorous, warring action of the Omaha spreading through the Indian territories, life for the tribe was very peaceful and productive in the years from 1850 to 1855. In this period, the Bellevue community grew in commerce and agriculture. The fertile area along the Missouri and Platte Rivers attracted many settlers who made their living by breaking the virgin soil and raising fowl and livestock. In constructing their homes, the farmers took many a cue from the Indians, erecting earthen lodges and soddies for warmth.

Traffic up the river from Saint Louis and Saint Joseph began to increase in the early 1850's, turning Bellevue from an outpost along the river to a churning, bustling river port of western civilization. Despite the activity along the river, the vast area to the west still remained a desolate wilderness occupied by an occasional herd of antelope or buffalo hunted by an occasional Indian hunting party. Life on this moor was hard and cruel. Few white men traversed the wind-swept prairie and none sought to carve out a living for themselves upon it.

In the Omaha village, competition existed among the various Christian denominations and the holy men of the tribe who were seeking to maintain the Indian religious values. Among the most influential men of the tribe in this endeavor was Black Bear, a powerful medicine man who many times resorted to spreading of superstition to hold the people within the sphere of Omaha religious beliefs. Black Bear sought to influence the stronger men of the tribe so that the lesser members would follow suit in listening to his teachings.

As part of his approach to Logan, Black Bear attempted to gain the chief's ear by appearing to look after his personal welfare.

On one of the holy days of the tribe, the birthday of chief Blackbird, the faithful, including Logan, gathered for the holy

Dance of the Spirits.   Following the ceremony, Black Bear approached Logan for conversation.

"Chief White Horse, in a recent meditation I had a vision which I feel obligated to tell you about.   In this vision I saw an angry wolf who was lying in the grass licking his wounds and waiting and waiting . . .   Along with this vision, I received a message that stated that I am to advise you against participating in any more hunts or battle operations to avoid meeting the wolf.   I am to warn you that if you ignore this message, it will prove fatal."

Realizing the scheming nature of Black Bear, Fontenelle scoffed at his words and walked toward his lodge leaving the medicine man singing a prayer for him in the dancing circle.

Logan, who was now thirty years of age, still was too young to take predictions of his death seriously.   The chief did not think much of the words of Black Bear until a weathered plainsman named William Brendt walked into the Omaha camp one day with a rifle in one hand and leading his horse with the other.   After watering his animal, the greying frontiersman sized up the village tipis and the young boys peering at him through very dark eyes.   Approaching the youngsters, the stranger asked: "Be there a chief here name of Fontenelle?"

Smiling, the wide-eyed boys just pointed to Logan's lodge. Brendt turned his horse around and led him past a long row of decorated tipis into chief's country and up to Big Elk's old lodgepole.   Tying his mount to the pole, Brendt rapped on the front support with his rifle.   When Logan appeared in the doorway, Brendt asked, "Are you the chief name of Fontenelle?"

"I am Logan Fontenelle, what is the problem?"

"Brendt is my name, and I've just gone through Sioux territory," said the tired-looking old scout.   "Some five weeks ago when I was passing through the hills about three hundred miles from here, I was stopped by an Oglala war party.   I think the only thing that saved my old hide was that I told their leader, a feller name of Sharp Horn, that I was headin' this way.   Why, when I told him I was a goin' to Bellevue, he acted like a man possessed by the devil himself. He gave me back my horse and rifle and told me I was free to go if I would deliver a message to Fontenelle. The message is that he would like to have a 'meeting of honor' with you. He says that he'll be waiting for you on the Beaver where the buffalo are the fattest."

Logan's face flushed with anger as he digested the old man's words. He then thanked the traveler and invited him to stay in the guest lodge where he would have a good bed and where the women of the tribe would cook his meals. Old Bill promptly accepted.

Logan retreated into the privacy of his lodge and reflected on Brandt's words and Sharp Horn's challenge. Perhaps there was something of substance in Black Bear's vision after all.

Logan was not the type of person who would jump at a challenge, nor was he the kind that shirked at the thought of facing a worthy opponent in combat. The thing that bothered him, however, was that out there in the desolate sandhills lurked a madman whose only objective in life was his destruction. After many hours of concentration on the subject, Logan decided that he would not honor the challenge and that he would not lend dignity to Sharp Horn by dwelling on it any longer. Certainly the affairs of the tribe commanded most of his attention and this was enough to occupy his mind.

In the spring of 1855, the Omaha women planted some very large fields of corn and supplemented the plant with plenty of squash, melons, and beans. Also, in the spring of the year the Omaha hunting parties managed to bring in an adequate supply of deer and some antelope. As spring and early summer wore on, however, the total area around Bellevue began to suffer from lack of rainfall and by midsummer the dry conditions turned into an extreme drought.

Despite the many Rain Dances that were held in order to convince Wakonda of the need for moisture, the efforts of the dancers fell on parched soil and as the corn tasseled, it withered away. The crop of squash and beans did no better than the corn and the total situation left the Omaha people in real trouble in preparing their food reserves for the winter.

At the meeting of the Council of Chiefs, the drought and the food supply were discussed. Unanimously, the chiefs voted that the tribe needed to supplant the loss in corn and other plant foods with buffalo meat. Hence, they planned a buffalo hunt in the sandhills for late summer. As hunt director, the chiefs picked Logan who had not served in this capacity before.

While the tribe prepared supplies, weapons, tipis, and travois for a month of hunting, Logan spent long hours praying for the success of the hunt. In his prayers he couldn't but wonder how the hunt might relate to the warning of Black Bear and the challenge of Sharp Horn. So, in this respect, Logan had a double reason to pray for bravery, strength, and guidance in his new responsibility for the tribe.

Despite the heat and dusty drought of August, 1855, the major portion of the Omaha people moved west and north early one day with only one purpose in mind--acquiring meat for the winter coffers. As was customary, Logan, the hunt director, followed on foot behind the tribe on the first day praying all the while for the success of the hunt.

With the summer heat worse than it had been in twenty years, the tribe traveled only five hours each day along the course of the Platte toward Buffalo country. Logan remained to himself and lived in his own tipi during the trek. Not even his closest friend and cousin, Iron Eye, approached him, since this was essential for the total success of the endeavor.

Slowly, the Omaha column reached a point where it left the Platte and turned toward the grassy sandhills. The Omaha passed several landmarks that were very significant to Logan and the rest of the braves who in their last trip to the sandhills were occupied by thoughts of clashes with Sioux war parties. The people didn't expect to meet any Sioux forces on this trip, however, because they felt the heat and the drought would keep them out of the arid, sandy area.

The heat and drought definitely entered into Logan's hunt plans. Instead of camping in the hills, Logan felt that his tribe would be more comfortable if they set up a permanent camp along Beaver Creek and launched their hunts from that point. The director's plans were realized when after eight days on the trail his scouts reported that they had reached the stream and it held running water.

The Omaha pitched their tipis along the Beaver at a point that is some five miles southwest of the present Nebraska town of Petersburg. Here the Omaha drank, bathed, and relaxed after a hot, dirty trip.

Logan sent out scouts in several directions on the morning of the tenth day to search for buffalo. All parties returned with nothing to report. This did not seem to disturb the tribe who continued to relax and bathe in the cool, spring-fed stream.

The next day, Logan sent a party of scouts to track upstream in the hope that the buffalo were also staying close to the water source. These scouts reported by early afternoon that they had sighted a medium-sized herd of bison along the creek some two miles away. This word excited all the members of the tribe and they began intense preparations for the move on the herd.

Before the sun rose on the next day, Logan picked two youths who were to proceed ahead of the hunting party carrying the sacred pipe. Once these youths left camp heading in the direction of the bison, the hunting party followed close behind. After the hunters came most of the women and young men riding or leading horses fitted with travois that eventually would carry the packs of meat obtained in the hunt.

The parties approached the grazing area slowly and cautiously. The boys out front looked carefully around each turn in the creek and over each hilltop so as not to startle the wary beasts.

It was still early morning when the boys climbed to the top of a ridge bordering the clear creek. Suddenly, they came to a halt and raised the sacred pipe as a signal to the hunters that the herd was in the valley next to the water. Here the boys separated to circle the herd as was the custom of the Omaha people.   The hunters readied their weapons and took their positions in the "surround" in a very quiet manner, but the heart of each of these young men was in his throat.   All waited for the signal from the hunt director to attack.   Once Logan could see that the boys were in a safe position away from the dangerous beasts, he gave his sign.

Without a yelp the Omaha hunters raced their steeds to close in on three sides of the unsuspecting herd of two hundred.   At first the huge animals were unshaken by the onslaught of hunters heading in their direction and they merely looked up from their feeding.   In a flash, however, the contented, docile herd turned into a wild, thundering mass.   The huge bulls seemed unstoppable as they gained momentum in the chase.   Steadily, the speedy ponies of the hunters slid alongside the rolling brown wave and drove arrow after arrow into the large racing hulks.   Before the chase had gone a half mile, many of the bulls had crashed into the ground kicking furiously until moaning their last breaths. The braves soon brought the hunt to an end after using up their arrows and twenty mound-like carcasses lay in the grass, the result of their efforts.

In wild delight, the women and boys moved into position to butcher the fallen bison.   They removed the tongues and hearts, which in their religious tradition would be the first tissue eaten by the tribe.   The job of butchering and wrapping the meat in the hides was completed by mid-afternoon.   The party stacked the packs on the travois and happily returned to the main camp. That night the people celebrated late, feasting on boiled tongue and heart and dancing by the light of fires made with buffalo chips and willow wood from along the stream.

The people kept very busy the following day salting and drying the meat harvest.   This was mandatory because the meat would not otherwise last in the extremely hot temperatures.

As the day dragged on, Fontenelle decided to find some secluded place to pray and thank Wakonda for the bountiful hunt.   Taking his shotgun, the chief mounted his horse and rode to the northwest toward a long high ridge capped with oak trees that overlooked a north-to-east bend in the creek. He felt that this would be an ideal site for meditation because it appeared cool and quiet.

Suddenly, as Logan approached the bend in the stream, he was confronted by three Indians on horseback, readily identified as Sioux. Many thoughts crossed his mind as he rode toward the trio who he could see were armed only with bows. Logan's main concern was not for his own safety, but for the security of the hunt. He knew that if one of the Sioux got away, the hunt would have to end, for soon the area would be crawling with enemy warriors. He had to kill all three of the Sioux.

As the chief closed on the trio near the water's edge, one of the colorfully painted warriors called to him: "I see you have honored my challenge, Fontenelle. It is time that the test of blood has been made between us." Immediately, Logan recognized his enemy as Sharp Horn. He knew that he probably could defeat the older Sharp Horn, but in no way could he overcome all three of the braves. Quickly, he cocked his shotgun and with a volley of lead from each barrel two of the braves were blown from their steeds and lay dying in the sand.

Sharp Horn charged his horse at the Omaha chief before Logan could reload. The horses collided and both riders were thrown from their mounts. They rose almost simultaneously from the sand facing each other with knives drawn. As they maneuvered for advantage, their actions carried them into the water. Fiercely, they slashed at each other; steel cut through the skin of both. Suddenly, Sharp Horn stumbled and lost his footing on the hard bottom of the creek and as he went down, Logan moved over him. Both stabbed wildly and the water ran red with Omaha and Sioux blood. From a squatting position in the water, Sharp Horn grabbed Logan's arm and pulled him into his knife. As Logan fell forward, however, his knife found its mark in the throat of the Sioux chief. The struggle was over. Logan picked himself up and stumbled toward the bank where he fell and died. The vision of the medicine man had become reality.

Iron Eye and several braves rode to the site of the duel after hearing the shotgun blasts. They looked upon the scene with disbelief as they viewed Sharp Horn face down in the water and Logan and the two Sioux braves lying in the blood-stained sand.

The braves tied Logan and his shotgun to his horse and the party guided their beloved chief back to his people.

In their total history, the Omaha people had seen much death and misery, but of all the depressing incidents they had experienced, they found this to be the worst. Logan was placed on a blanket in the tipi of the White Buffalo and the women of the hunt began their wailing vigil while a lone drummer began beating out a melancholy cadence just outside. The men and boys of the tribe all stood in shock as they took their turns throughout the night viewing their fallen leader. Many of the braves gashed themselves with their knives in grief.

The tribe packed for their long, sad trek back to Bellevue at sunrise. Logan was wrapped tightly in a buffalo robe and strapped to a travois for the trip which took eight days to complete. Stories that have been passed along through the years state that when the tribe reached their home village, the death bundle holding the chief reeked from the odor of rancid flesh, but this did not deter the people from giving their hero a proper burial.

Unwritten tales of the burial state that Logan was placed with his shotgun in an unmarked grave which was to be kept secret forever by his people. To this day it has not been discovered.

Despite the monuments that have been erected to Fontenelle since his death, they did not supplant his presence. The Omaha, though very proud warriors, never fully recovered from the emptiness of Logan's passing.

It was finished! Logan Fontenelle was dead. In his few young years, he accomplished what the great chiefs and combined hordes of the Comanche, Cheyenne, and Arapaho could not accomplish. He had blunted the ambitions of some of the most powerful tribes of the plains and never again did that menace challenge the peaceful people along the Missouri.

Postscript

The factual version of the life of Logan Fontenelle states that Logan was the oldest of the half-breed sons of Lucien Fontenelle, a noted French fur-trader, and Bright Sun, the daughter of Big Elk, a famous and powerful chief of the Omaha tribe in the 1800's. During Big Elk's reign, the Omaha lived near the outpost of Bellevue, Nebraska, the gateway to the West for the trappers, adventurers, missionaries, and hunters who opened up the new land.

Lucien Fontenelle operated the fur-trading post for the American Fur Company in Bellevue and at the time he built a good home for his family nearby. Bellevue was also the site of the Indian Agency for the area and this brought a variety of Indian tribes to Bellevue.

Since he lived in Bellevue and because of his famous father, Logan became good friends with many notable people who traveled through the area. Some of his associates were Kit Carson, Prince Maximilian, Karl Bodmer, George Catlin, Brigham Young and the Mormans, and Father Pierre DeSmet, the "Blackrobe."

Father DeSmet became very well known because he was the first missionary to carry the message of Christ to some of the fierce, heathen tribes in Nebraska, the Dakotas, and Montana. He spent the major part of his career working with these tribes and occasionally he served as a peace moderator during their wars with one another.

When Logan was in his teens, he was taken by DeSmet to the Jesuit secondary school near St. Louis where he received a two-year education. He returned to Bellevue at the death of his father and because of the influence of his mother, he became heavily involved in the activities of the Omaha tribe. At the death of Big Elk, Logan and his cousin Joseph La Flesche (Iron Eye) were inducted into the Council of Chiefs, which ruled the tribe.

Most of the smaller and weaker tribes of eastern Nebraska, including the Omaha, were constantly harassed by the Sioux tribes whenever they moved to hunt buffalo in the sandhills to the west. Once Logan and Iron Eye reached chiefdom, they decided that they would no longer tolerate harassment from the Sioux. On at least three occasions while hunting buffalo in what is now Boone County, Nebraska, the Omaha engaged the Sioux and each time inflicted severe punishment upon them. Because of his intelligence and his leadership in skirmishes with the Sioux, Logan, though young, was heralded as somewhat of a "messiah" among his people. Under his direction the Omaha had regained their self-respect.

In 1855 the Omaha moved to their new reservation near Decatur, Nebraska. Since it was a bad year for their crops, the tribe decided to conduct a buffalo hunt to supply their food coffers. Logan, who was thirty years old at the time, was chosen as director of the hunt. Moving west from Decatur, the Omaha crossed the Elkhorn River and then moved in a southwesterly direction. When close to the site of present-day Petersburg, Nebraska they sighted elk and Logan, Iron Eye, and a brave named Sansouci took chase. In their move on the elk, Logan became separated from the other two hunters. Iron Eye and Sansouci, while engaged in pursuit, observed a large band of Sioux approaching so they retreated back to the main body of Omaha. The Sioux then surrounded the Omaha and a battle ensued that lasted several hours.

Several versions exist about what happened to Fontenelle after he became separated from Iron Eye and Sansouci, but it is known that he also had an encounter with the Sioux and was killed.

When the Sioux withdrew from their attack on the Omaha party, some of Logan's friends went in search of him along Beaver Creek. They found his body with seven arrows in the chest and with a crushed skull from a tomahawk blow. Logan had been armed with a double-barreled gun and evidence showed that at least one Sioux had a large portion of his body shot away by the Omaha chief.

The Omaha braves wrapped Logan in buckskin and transported him on the back of a mule to Bellevue for burial. When they reached Logan's home his body reeked terribly and was so swollen it would not fit in a coffin built by his brother. On the day of burial, two weeks after his death, large numbers of people participated in the ceremony conducted by Stephen Decatur.

Today it is not known where Logan is buried. It is not known whether he lies in the family plot in Fontenelle Forest at Bellevue or if he lies separately in a secret grave alongside his double-barreled gun.

Author's Note

Eventually all of the western Indian tribes succumbed to the onslaught of the white man's western migration. One by one the great tribes were overcome and the survivors were placed on reservations to vegetate on marginal land away from the path of the expansion of civilization as we know it. Oh, what a different story could have unfolded had some of the redmen refused to assist the whites in their trips west or if the Indians had forgotten their tribal feuds and banded together to oppose the western movement.

Today the plight of the original American on reservations is a disgrace to a nation that supposedly is concerned with human rights. Many people of the original tribes lie mired in the muck of poverty, enslaved in a system of government dependence from which there is no promise. Most Americans care little about the proud history of the Indian or what the future holds for these people. Authors write little about them and publishers are not interested in telling their story, concerning themselves mostly with the problems of other minorities, with success stories of entertainers or athletes, or with stories of the European holocaust.

The account of the redman, who lost his land and who today finds himself exiled within it, is another holocaust about which little will ever be mentioned. Only when the Indian, his philosophy, and his customs have been absorbed within our total society will someone realize what existed and what has been lost forever.